A Price Above Rubies

By

Merline Lovelace

copyright@merlinelovelace

First Edition - June 2021

Chronology

1187, October - Pope Gregory VIII calls for a Third Crusade to recapture the Holy Land from Saladin

1188, January - Phillip of France and Henry II of England end their war with each other and take the Cross; both impose a "Saladin Tithe" to raise money for their Crusade. Henry's son Richard, known as Lionheart, also takes the Cross.

1188, March - Henry Barbarossa of Germany takes the Cross, organizes his army, and departs for the Holy Land in April, 1189

1189, July - Henry II of England dies and is succeeded by his son Richard

1189, August - Richard arrives in England

1189, September - Richard crowned king and sets about raising men and money for his Crusade

1190, June - Richard and Phillip of France join forces and depart for the Holy Land

1191, August - Phillip returns to France, begins attacking Richard's holdings

1192, October - Richard negotiates a truce with Saladin and departs the Holy Land to reclaim his lands

1192, December - Richard taken captive on his way home by Leopold of Austria

1194, February - Richard released after his mother, Queen Eleanor, raises exorbitant ransom

1194 -1198 - Richard fights to regain his lost lands while still determined to return to the Holy Land and retake Jerusalem.

1199, March - Richard wounded at siege of Chalus, dies on April 2nd

Chapter One

Exmoor Keep, on the River Alyn
A holding in the Western Marches
July 1189

"My lord!"

When the shout rang down from the watch tower that hot summer afternoon, Hugh Montmercy, Baron Exmoor, lord of Bellemeade, Charlney, and Pontvieu keeps, as well as a half dozen lesser holdings in England and on the continent, felt no prickle of unease, no sense of foreboding that his life was about to take a course he'd neither anticipated nor desired. Still less that his lust for a stubborn, flame-haired wench would bring them both to the brink of disaster. His only thought at the time was to answer the sentry's call without cleaving his opponent through the helmet.

Halting his sword in mid-swing, he signaled the young squire he was training to step back. When the huffing, sweat-soaked lad dropped his sword, Hugh turned his attention to the watch tower.

"Aye?"

"The troop you sent to Chester approaches."

Hugh's brows hooked in surprise. He'd dispatched the troop just four days ago. They were to escort the distant kinswoman who'd sent a missive to his mother requesting shelter at Exmoor. He hadn't expected them to return so quickly, especially in these unsettled times.

"Do you see their pennant?"

"Aye, m'lord. They fly the eagle of Exmoor."

"Very well. Allow them entry. And you," he said to his panting young opponent, "find Lady Alice and tell her Eleanor de Brac approaches."

As the lad scurried off, Hugh dragged up the hem of his linen shirt to wipe his face and neck. He'd worked up a healthy sweat, and the hot summer sun beat down brightly. When he lowered his shirttail, he spotted his youngest brother darting across the yard. Guy snatched up the squire's sword and swished it through the air with all the vigor of his eight years. "Will you show me that neck thrust, brother?"

"Why are you not at your lessons?"

Hugh already knew the answer. Guy would as lief suck a turnip as spend an hour deciphering Latin texts with the castle priest.

"It's too fair a day to stay inside."

Unrepentant, the boy grinned. He was a tall, strapping lad, with a shock of hair the same saddle brown as the rest of the Montmercy clan. Hugh should have sent him to another lord's household for fostering a year ago. The boy was up for every lark and as like to be in trouble as out of it. He needed a stern overlord who wouldn't hesitate to clout him alongside the head when necessary.

More to the point, the alliances formed by such fostering were the threads that wove the fabric of the ever-shifting balance of power among the barons who ruled the borderlands between England and Wales. Hugh himself had fostered with the earl of Chester and had served as squire to the great William Marshal.

He'd arranged a good place for Guy, as well, but his lady mother was loathe to send off the last of her chicks. So Hugh had indulged her wish to keep him with her one more year, just as he'd indulged her when she'd asked him to provide shelter for this distant kinswoman. Although Lady Alice knew little about the woman - only that she was the spinster daughter of a distant cousin by marriage - Hugh had agreed to her request readily enough. What was one more female in a household that contained so many ladies-in-waiting, widows, and well-born girls sent to Lady Alice for tutelage?

He only hoped the captain of the guard he'd sent to escort the woman hadn't rattled her bones by pushing too hard and too fast. His mother would not be best pleased. Lady Alice's heart had near melted when she'd learned that this elderly kinswoman had journeyed all the way from Outremer with only a young female charge as companion.

Well, his mother would see to the woman's comfort, and Hugh would welcome her himself tonight at supper. In the meantime he would instruct his brother in the fine art of skewering an opponent through the neck.

"Very well, Guy. Take up a shield and…"

"Sir Hugh!"

The bellow this time came from the captain of the guard. Silhouetted against the bright sunlight, the man beckoned vigorously from the square watchtower.

"You'd best come and look on this."

The urgent request sent Hugh striding for the stairs, Guy hard on his heels. With the Old King, Henry II, dead less than a month and the as-yet-uncrowned Richard Lionheart fighting to subdue rebellious vassals in Normandy, tension simmered near to boiling among the fiercely independent barons of the Western marches. Those who had remained loyal to Henry in his war against his sons would now have to answer to Richard for their actions. Those who'd sided with the son against the father waited to be rewarded for their loyalty. Then there were those who believed Richard's nephew, Arthur, should rule by right of primogeniture.

Only the indomitable will of Queen Eleanor, newly released from more than sixteen years of imprisonment by her husband, held the English barons at bay. But old feuds and greedy expectations now ripped at the tangled web of alliances among the border lords. Each day it became more difficult to know friend from potential foe. Fully prepared to order the drawbridge raised and issue a call to arms, Hugh gained the rampart with Guy hard on his heels.

"What's amiss?"

"I'm not certain," the captain of his guard replied, gesturing to a distant plume of dust.

At first glance Hugh saw no reason for alarm. The party raising that dust was indeed the troop he'd sent to escort the expected visitor. Exmoor's eagle fluttered from the lead horseman's pike. The rest of the escort rode at a leisurely pace before and behind a wheeled litter.

Suddenly a flash of sunlight on burnished metal caught Hugh's eye. The next moment two riders burst from a screen of bracken. Near neck and neck, they raced along the dirt road leading to massive earthen mound topped by Exmoor Keep.

Hugh squinted at the device on the surcoat and shield of one rider. "That's Sir Giles."

"Aye, milord. But the other…"

"The other is a female!" Guy burst out, scrunching into a squint for a better look.

Christ's wounds! It was a female. Young and slender, from the look of her. Her veil and skirts aflutter, she lay almost across the neck of her mount.

Hugh's heart catapulted into his throat. This must be the youthful charge accompanying the elderly cousin. What was Giles about to mount the girl atop such a spirited animal instead of a well-mannered palfrey? The damned thing must have bolted and run away with her.

He saw the error of his thinking mere moments later, when the rider's veil blew into her face. Gathering the reins into one hand, she ripped off the offending headdress with the other, threw it aside and urged her mount into a burst of speed that left Giles in the dust.

"By the knuckles of Saint John," Guy muttered in awe as horse and rider pounded toward the keep, "but look at that courser!"

"I see it," Hugh replied grimly.

Anger that the maid would so recklessly outdistance her escort warred with admiration for her mount. The animal was magnificent! African, obviously, bred for speed and endurance in the desert. The king of Naples had crossed coursers such as that one with European breeds and now sold them for nigh onto a prince's ransom.

Horse and rider were forced to slow to avoid the chickens and pigs rooting in the dirt in the village at the base of the hill. But they regained speed on the long slope leading up to the keep, left bare for defensive purposes. Moments later they drummed across the bridge spanning the moat with a thunder of hooves on wood.

Their precipitous arrival turned the heads of every man-at-arms, stable lad, and servant in the bailey. Even the smith left his forge to gawk at the prancing, curveting steed. As Hugh descended from the ramparts, his eyes were on its rider. She looked to be somewhat older than he'd first thought. Eighteen, mayhap, or thereabouts. Slender and supple, but round of hip and firm of back.

Certainly, she was no maid or serving girl. Her gown was cut in a style long out of favor with Hugh's mother and sisters but richly adorned with embroidery. Unfettered by veil or circlet, her wind-tossed hair glowed in the afternoon sun like copper heated in the smithy's forge. Then she twisted in her saddle, and Hugh's breath left on a muttered oath.

"*Jesu!*"

She wasn't a beauty. The sun had bronzed her face and throat to an unbecoming hue. Her mouth was too wide, her chin too firm without a wimple to soften its bold lines. But by the saints, she blazed with life!

Eyes sparking, cheeks flushed, she shoved back her disordered hair and called out to the knight only now clattering across the drawbridge. "A good race, Sir Giles! Sirocco and I thank you for the chance to stretch our legs."

Hugh's chief vassal drew rein alongside her. Below the nosepiece of his helmet, his usually dour mouth was stretched in a wide grin. "That beast is well and truly named. He flies like the hot winds of the desert."

"That he does."

"Hold, and I'll help you dismount."

Recalled to their duties, the stable boys rushed to take the reins and assist the heavily mailed knight from his saddle. Hugh himself came forward to do the same for the female astride the magnificent stallion. The courser took exception to his approach and kicked out with his hooves.

"Back, man!"

The woman's sharp order brought a chorus of gasps from the onlookers. None of Hugh's people would dare speak to him in such a tone.

"Sirocco does not know you," she said briskly. "Nor does he need a hand on the reins. He will stand to my command."

Murmuring something in a strange language, she kicked her right foot free of the stirrup, brought her left over the cantle and slid gracefully from the saddle. Hugh caught a glimpse of much-darned stocking and a red boot with a long, curled toe. Another murmured command brought down the steed's narrow, fine-boned head. Flicking the reins over his silky, snow-white mane, she offered them to Hugh.

"Now you may take him. Groom him well, if you please. He especially likes to have his legs rubbed with weven hay."

The startled silence this produced was broken by a hoot from young Guy. "Ha, brother! She thinks you a varlet."

And small wonder, Hugh acknowledged wryly. Sweat plastered his shirt to his back. The tails hung over equally sweat-stained leather breeks. Having spent an hour in the kennels before joining the squires at training, he didn't doubt he carried the stink of dogs.

The lady cocked her head at Guy's unrestrained glee. Turning her gaze once more to

Hugh, she looked him up and down. The speculative gleam in her eyes made him feel much like a stallion being considered as stud.

God's bones, she was a bold wench! Would that he *could* service her as a stallion would a mare.

As quickly as the thought leapt into his head, he shoved it out. She and the elderly woman she'd accompanied across the seas were now his responsibility. Hugh had many faults, but he'd never abused a woman under his protection.

"I sense I mistake the matter," she said with a rueful smile. "You are not one of the groomsmen?"

"No, no!" Sir Giles rounded his horse and hurried toward them, his chainmail clinking. "This is my liege, the lord of Exmoor."

Contrary to Hugh's expectations, the lady neither colored in dismay nor stammered an apology. Instead she laughed merrily and stretched out her hand once more.

"Then you *must* take the reins, sir. Sirocco is yours, brought from Outremer as a gift for your generosity in agreeing to shelter a homeless kinswoman and her charge. I hope he meets with your approval."

How could he not? The courser's head was small and finely shaped, with large, dark eyes and firm jowls. His deep chest, well-sprung ribs, and large joints showed he was bred for strength as well as speed. As enthralled by the horse as by the woman who'd delivered it, Hugh accepted the reins.

"Sirocco, is it?"

"Aye, my lord."

Ears pricked forward, eyes wary, the courser allowed the stranger to stroke its velvety muzzle. After a moment, he nickered softly and blew into Hugh's palm. Horse and man became one at that moment.

"I thank you," Hugh said gruffly, "as I will thank your mistress when she arrives with the rest of the troop."

"My mistress?"

"You travel with Eleanor de Brac, do you not?"

Giles intervened once more. "Your pardon, lord. This is the lady you sent me to escort."

Hugh's gaze whipped back to the copper-haired female. "*You* are Eleanor de Brac?"

"I am." Her green eyes danced with laughter, inviting him to share in the jest. "It would appear we each mistook the other."

"So it would," he said dryly.

His lady mother had searched her memory after receiving the unexpected and most surprising missive from Outremer. As best Lady Alice could recall, she'd met Simon de Brac but once, at her betrothal ceremony to his cousin. She remembered him as a blustery, boastful third son, prone to drink or gamble away whatever prizes he won in battle or at tourneys. Her husband had expressed only relief when he related that his cousin had decided to go on Crusade and seek his fortune in distant lands.

That was more than four decades ago. None had seen or heard from de Brac since, as he'd chosen to stay on in the Levant and hire out his sword to the Latin kings of Jerusalem. Lady Alice had been surprised to learn he'd taken a wife, even more surprised that he'd sired a daughter who could compose such a pretty missive.

She'd tried to guess the daughter's age. Thirty, mayhap? Or closer to forty, if de Brac had wed soon after his arrival in the Levant. Why he'd not found a husband for this daughter was a puzzle. She must have a terrible squint, his mother had mused. Or, God forbid, she'd inherited her sire's unfortunate beak of a nose.

The smiling young woman now standing before Hugh put paid to those dire speculations. She showed no trace of a squint. Sported no hooked nose. Her shabby raiment suggested she'd inherited little in material goods from either parent, but Hugh guessed she would not remain husbandless much longer. Her lithe body and laughing eyes would tempt many a man to overlook her poor estate. And, Hugh decided, he would sweeten the pot with an appropriate dower. It was the least he could do in exchange for the magnificent gift she'd brought him. Stroking Sirocco's muzzle a final time, he summoned his head groom.

"Tend him well. He especially likes to have his legs rubbed with weven hay," he added with a twitch of his lips.

The sight of that half smile curled Eleanor's toes inside her Moroccan leather boots. Holy Virgin! Did the lord of Exmoor have any notion how that mere hint of laughter altered his aspect and demeanor?

She'd taken him for one of the lower orders when he'd first approached. Big and well-muscled, as befitted a lord's groom or man-at-arms, but weathered and uncouth. Even after learning his identity, she'd not been overly impressed. Hugh of Exmoor, she'd decided, was too stern of face, too stiff and formal for her tastes.

Ah, but when he smiled – or almost smiled! – the years fell off him. He looked younger and every bit as intriguing as the youth he now made known to her as his brother, Guy. The boy's bright blue eyes enchanted her, as did his awkward bow. She was returning his greeting when the rattle of hooves on the drawbridge announced the arrival of her escort.

Oh, Lud! The fat would be in the fire now. Squaring her shoulders, Eleanor braced herself for the storm she knew would come.

Sure enough, a small and most vociferous dervish erupted from the litter almost before its wheels had ceased to turn.

"A pox on you, Ella!" she said angrily.

The girl possessed the midnight black hair and warm skin of the desert peoples. But, like Eleanor, had inherited their sire's sea-green eyes. At the moment, those seas were stormy indeed.

Stalking across the bailey, the six-year-old poured out a torrent of Latin, Arabic and the Italian favored at the court of the kings of Jerusalem. "*Sancta Maria!* You leave me to jounce about in this thrice-damned donkey cart. You have the breeze in your face while I choke on dust. You ride like the wind, and I…"

"French, Jasmine. You must speak the French of Normandy now."

"Pah!" She flung up a hand, her bracelets jangling. "French is for pigs. I cannot get my tongue around such grunts and snorts."

"Nonetheless, you must endeavor to do so."

Warned by the mutinous set to the girl's mouth, Eleanor softened her tone. Honey always worked better with Jasmine than vinegar. "Be sweet, like the flower you are named for, and let me make you known to the lord of this keep."

"Then do it quickly, for I must piss. The wagon, it bounces and jounces me like…"

"Yes, yes, I know."

Praying the girl wouldn't squat and relieve herself on the spot, Eleanor addressed her host. "Sir Hugh, this is my half-sister, Jasmine."

The girl executed a passable curtsey. Then, being Jasmine, she planted her hand on the hilt of her jeweled dagger, craned her neck, and matched Exmoor stare for stare.

It was as if a whippet faced a bear, Eleanor thought in mingled pride and exasperation. One so small and fearless, the other so tall and fearsome.

"Jasmine," she chided. "Give your greeting."

"*Ave*, my lord. My sister and I, we are most grateful to take shelter with you and your lady."

Eleanor breathed a sigh of relief that she'd remembered the words they'd rehearsed. Young Guy, however, had no interest in such civilities. His avid gaze was fixed on Jasmine's dagger.

"Is that a Saracen blade?"

"It is," the girl replied with a haughty tilt to her chin, "and made of the finest Damascus steel."

"How did you come by it?"

"My father…" Her voice faltered. Gulping, she fingered the jeweled hilt. "My father gifted me with it before he dies."

Eleanor's heart twisted. She, too, missed their scapegrace sire. Despite his complete disregard for any comfort but his own, Simon de Brac had been as generous of heart as he was with his purse. Not that his purse had ever contained more than a few sous. Whatever he earned by hiring out his sword he spent freely on wine, dicing, and dancing girls. Luck invariably ran against him, however. Including the time he'd wagered his armor, shield and destrier for the sullen slave girl who'd caught his fancy. Just days after birthing their babe, the girl had disappeared into the desert.

Her flight had left Eleanor with the task of raising her half-sister as well as managing her father's often chaotic household. Then, last year, Simon had taken an arrow intended for the sultan he'd hired his sword to. Eleanor still felt the loss but at least she had Jasmine to alternately madden and delight her. The tie between the sisters was stronger than any steel ever forged in Damascus.

Which was why they'd left what remained of the war ravaged Kingdom of Jerusalem. Why they'd traveled so long and so far. It wasn't safe in the East. Not with the Saracens battling so fiercely to take back the lands wrested from them in the second great Crusade. Nor had Eleanor found a husband suitable to her needs among the ragtag knights and mercenaries clinging to the rapidly shrinking Christian court.

Find one she must, however. And soon. She ached to give Jasmine a safe, secure home after the turbulence of her early years. And truth be told, Eleanor herself had been plagued by the most sinful cravings these past few years. She was ready to taste the delights of the marriage bed. More than ready! And for that she must needs have a husband. One she could manage with the same ease she'd managed her sire. But younger, of course, and strong and well-muscled.

Like Hugh of Exmoor.

As her gaze roamed over him once more, heat stirred in her belly. He was much a man, this stern-faced baron of the Marches. Very much a man. Wondering how it would feel to have arms roped with such sinewy muscles enfold her, she barely heard the patter of hurried footsteps.

"Hugh! What are you about, keeping our guests here in the hot sun?"

Two women crossed the outer bailey in a flurry of silks and veils. One was young and garbed in an elegantly cut lavender bliaut that stirred instant envy in Eleanor's breast. The other, she guessed at once, must be Lady Alice. Age had carved fine lines at the older woman's eyes and mouth, but the brown strands that escaped her linen headdress had traces of the same gold as that of her sons. And her eyes, although somewhat faded by age, were the same summer-sky blue.

"Forgive me, lady mother. Your guests arrived but moments since." With a courteous gesture, Exmoor indicated Eleanor. "If it pleases you, I would make known Eleanor de Brac, the daughter of your cousin by marriage."

Lady Alice's eyes popped beneath her linen veil. "*You* are Simon's daughter?"

Clearly they had expected a middle-aged spinster, not the product of a mismatch between a rag-tag knight and lady more than thirty years his junior. Biting the inside of her cheek to hold back her laughter, Eleanor dropped a curtsey and confirmed her person for the second time.

"I am Eleanor."

"But I thought… I was sure…"

"Aye," her son drawled. "So were we all."

Recovering her dignity, Lady Alice took Eleanor's hands in hers. "You are welcome, lady. I met your father but once, at my betrothal ceremony. As best I recall, Simon was a brave knight."

"Yes, he was."

Except when he was in his cups, Eleanor thought wryly. Then he was exceedingly foolish.

"And this is my sister, Jasmine."

"You are welcome, as well, Jasmine." If Lady Alice was surprised by Eleanor's relationship to a child with such warm skin and dark hair, she hid it well. "You must both be weary after your long journey. I'll instruct the kitchen maids to heat water for you to wash. Catherine, will you show our guests to the women's solar?"

The young girl at her side blushed and dipped her chin. "Aye, lady mother. This way, if you please."

Despite her rich raiment, the girl was painfully shy. She kept her head down and her eyes averted as she led the newcomers across the bailey. Still sulky from her long confinement inside the litter, Jasmine said little but Eleanor tried to engage the other girl in conversation and ease her shyness.

"You called Lady Alice mother. Are you sister to Sir Hugh?"

"Would that I *were!*"

Her vehement reply seemed to startle her as much as it did Eleanor. Something close to panic flooded her brown eyes. Throwing a frightened look over her shoulder, she dropped her voice to a ragged whisper.

"I am his wife."

Chapter Two

Exerting a visible effort to recover her poise, Lady Catherine fought for a timid smile. "Sir Hugh and I gave our vows nigh onto two years ago. I... I have been in his keeping since."

"In his keeping? Ah, I understand. Your vows were *verba de futuro*."

"Aye."

So the girl was bound to Exmoor, and he to her, by a promise to consummate their union in the future. It was a common enough practice when the bride was not yet twelve, the age the Church decreed acceptable for bedding and breeding. Such vows, Eleanor knew, were as binding as those made *verba de praesenti* and gave the husband all legal rights over his promised wife and her properties.

"This way," Catherine said as she led Eleanor past stables, kennels, and kitchens.

Exmoor Keep loomed ahead, solid and square in the Norman style. Constructed, Eleanor guessed, of stone quarried from the hills cut by the broad, flat river she and her escort had followed from Chester. Towers with arrow slits bristled at each of the keep's four corners. The curtain wall that encircled the castle and it yards was thick and looked nigh on impregnable.

The stairs leading to the keep's single entrance were constructed of wood, so they might be burned to deny an enemy entry, and perilously steep. Lifting her skirts, Catherine labored up the steps. The man-at-arms posted by the door sprang to open it for her. Cool, dank air trapped by the stone walls rushed out to greet the women as they stepped inside.

Eleanor looked around her with great interest. She had managed her father's household since she'd put away her rag dolls. She could stretch a sou until it squealed and haggle in the bazaar until wine sellers and cloth merchants tore their beards and cried that she stole the figs from their children's mouths. She'd also spent a good number of hours with the lesser ladies at the court of the kings of Jerusalem. Although etiquette was somewhat relaxed in the searing heat of the East, rank and privilege still held sway. Eleanor was well aware of her low estate, and never more so than when attending some feast or banquet to which the lesser knights and their ladies were invited.

So she knew from the moment she stepped into the keep's great hall that its lord was one of consequence. The tapestries adorning the walls shimmered with rich, jewel-like colors and the candles set in holders throughout the cavernous hall were as thick around as a man's thigh. The rushes strewn across the floors smelled of spilled beer, grease and dogs but didn't carry the stink of excrement so prevalent in many great houses.

A winding stair – tight and narrow to prevent attackers from being able to wield their swords – led to the upper floors. The chapel, knights' quarters, and lord's chamber occupied the second story, Lady Catherine informed the two guests. The ladies' solar and servants' quarters took up the third. Large and bright and sunny, the solar echoed with the clack of tapestry looms and the high, sweet notes of a singer accompanying herself on a lute.

"We've readied this spot for you," Catherine said, drawing aside a curtain to display a wall niche containing a wood-framed bed. "We had the mattress stuffed with extra straw. We thought… That is, we feared…"

"That my ancient bones would ache from the long journey," Eleanor finished, laughing. "And so they do, lady. I swear, we were lashed by every storm at sea and came near to being taken by pirates several times."

"Pirates!" Young Catherine's face went as pale as her linen headdress. "Do not say so!"

"Oh, aye. The rogues grow ever more bold with so many ships carrying pilgrims and crusaders to plunder."

"Weren't you terrified?"

"I chewed my knuckle once or twice," Eleanor admitted.

"I did not," Jasmine announced, bouncing on the mattress to test its plumpness. "I keep my dagger with me always. Any man who dared to touch Eleanor would have lost his hand or his fingers or his nose. Or his ballocks, could I get to them. Or mayhap his…"

The appearance of two servants bearing their traveling chests put an end to Jasmine's bloodthirsty recital. Lady Alice appeared soon after, accompanied by maids with leather buckets of hot water and bowls of soft soap.

Washed, combed and much refreshed, the two sisters were introduced to the other females in the bower. A goodly number, Eleanor saw with relief, were young girls near to Jasmine's age. The others included several unmarried maids pledged to knights in Exmoor's service, wives of various vassals, and numerous widowed aunts, nieces and cousins by marriage. She and Jasmine would not lack for company, Eleanor thought, as she tried to fix names to faces.

"We brought gifts for you and your ladies," she told Lady Alice. "Mere trifles, to thank you for your kindness in offering us shelter, but we hope they will please you. Shall I have Jasmine fetch them now?"

Lady Alice's kind heart turned at the unexpected generosity. She'd recovered from the shock of learning that her long-forgotten cousin-by-marriage had produced such a young, vivacious daughter and felt only sorrow that he'd left the girl in such poor estate. Her gown was such that the servants would deign to use it only for rags and her strange shoes with their curled toes showed much wear.

"You have no need to gift us, child. I am – we are all – most happy to have your company. Just hearing your tales of the East will be pleasure enough for us all."

That was certainly true. Minstrels, tinkers, and itinerant monks were greeted with great delight for the news they brought, as were knights returning from service abroad. To have someone fresh from Outremer here among them was enough to still the ladies' looms and have them scoot their stools closer.

"Hear them you shall," Eleanor promised, "but first you must let us share what we brought. Jasmine, sweet, fetch the bag containing the gifts."

While her sister did her bidding, Eleanor settled on a folding stool and looked at the colorful flock gathered around her. Her first chore, she thought, would to be sew new gowns for herself and her sister. She could see the ones they wore were sadly out of date.

Returning with the silken bag, Jasmine untied the drawstrings and drew out a thick fold of cloth.

"That is for you, Lady Alice," Eleanor said with a smile. "Happily, the color matches your eyes."

When Jasmine shook out the length of gossamer silk threaded with silver, the other women gasped in delight. Lady Alice, however, issued an instant protest. "I cannot accept such a gift! The cloth is far too fine and costly. You must save it to use as your dower."

"I'm dowered sufficient for my needs," Eleanor assured her, "as is Jasmine."

Overcoming the older woman's objections, she pressed the cloth on her and bid Jasmine dig into the sack once more. The rich scent of cinnamon spiced the air when the girl drew out a bundle of sticks tied with a ribbon.

These Eleanor presented to the stout matron Lady Alice had introduced as wife of Sir Giles, Exmoor's chief vassal and steward of this keep. While the other ladies ooohed and aaahed and sniffed the cinnamon, she passed a small, two handled cup of abalone shell carved with exotic symbols to young woman perched on a padded bench.

"For you, Lady Catherine."

A rosy blush tinted the girl's cheeks. Thanking Eleanor profusely, she turned the cup round and round. "It's most fine. Where does it come from?"

"Cathay, I think. I cannot read the symbols, but I'm told they express a wish for long life, much happiness, and many sons."

"S…sons?"

The delight drained from girl's eyes. She threw a quick look at Lady Alice, who answered it with a pointed one of her own.

"Aye," the older woman said firmly. "Sons. And many of them."

Catherine flinched. Her cheeks lost their rosy color and her voice was small when she whispered, "Yes, lady mother."

With a barely repressed sigh, Lady Alice returned her attention to Eleanor and Jasmine. By the time the sisters had given out the last of their gifts, the sunlight slanted through the windows at a sharp angle. The women dispersed to put away their sewing and prepare for dinner while Lady Alice went to oversee the laying of the boards. Catherine followed in her wake.

Her brow furrowed, Eleanor watched the two make for the stairs. Simon de Brac would have recognized his daughter's expression and immediately retreated to the nearest wine shop.

Eleanor tried to tell herself Lady Catherine was no concern of hers. Surely the girl had a father or brothers or an overlord to see to her welfare and protect her interests. But her obvious terror of marriage to Hugh of Exmoor stirred Eleanor's pity.

That came hard up against Eleanor's own reaction to the man. She'd never felt such a sudden, unexpected flush of heat. Which told her it was best she'd decided to go about the business she'd come for, and quickly.

With that thought in mind, she sent a page to find the lord of Exmoor and ask if she might beg the favor of storing a small casket in his strong room. While she waited for the page to return, she tugged at the thin silver chain circling her neck. The smith who'd forged it had reinforced the links as she'd directed and made the chain long enough that the key it held dangled securely between her breasts. She used the key to unlock the casket and extracted a small stone, which she wrapped in a handkerchief and tucked in the pocket of her gown.

The page returned a few moments later. "Sir Hugh awaits you in the counting room, lady."

Nodding, Eleanor hefted the casket under her arm and descended four flights of narrow, winding stairs to the nether regions.

The cellar was dank and windowless, sunk deep into the earthen mound that supported the keep. Dungeons and an armory with racks of pikes, spears, and bows took up most of the vaulted basement, storage rooms the rest. Even in high summer, the thick walls gave off a chill – an unfortunate state of affairs for the miscreants sentenced to the dungeons but ideal for preserving the hams and wild game and other foodstuffs that hung from hooks in the storerooms.

"This way, lady."

Elle followed the page along the central passageway, breathing in the odors of onions, pungent cheeses, and well-oiled leather hauberks. From behind a thick door came the perfume of pepper, ginger and cloves.

The chatelaine in Eleanor approved the stout lock on the spice room. The little bundle of cinnamon sticks she'd given to Sir Giles' wife had cost only a few sous in Eastern bazaars. Here, she knew, such spices were difficult to obtain and thus far more dear. A pound of ginger would buy a sheep, or so she'd been told. A cow could be had for a similar amount of mace. Pepper was so valuable that dockworkers' pockets were stitched shut so they couldn't steal a single peppercorn when they unloaded ships from the East. No fool, Eleanor had long suspected the great kings of Europe went on Crusade as much to keep the spice trade routes open as to secure the Holy Lands for devout pilgrims.

Eleanor couldn't help marveling at the vagaries of fate that had taken Simon de Brac to the East so many years ago and had now brought his daughter back across the seas.

"Here, lady."

The page stood aside to allow her entry into a counting room furnished with a table, two chairs, and rows of sturdy chests. As promised, Sir Hugh was waiting for her. A very different Sir Hugh than the one Eleanor had encountered in the yards!

She'd thought him much a man in sweat-stained shirt and breeks. In embroidered mantle, a knee-length tunic of fine wool and tight fitting chausses, he raised a silly flutter in her breast. Light from the tall candles burnished the subtle gold streaks his hair to a shine every bit as bright as the bezants minted by the Crusaders. His chin was strong and freshly pumiced free of bristles, his blue eyes polite.

"You wished to store something, lady?"

Recalled to her mission, Eleanor proffered the casket. "If you would, sir, keep this safe for me."

"Gladly."

She thought he might inquire as to its contents, but he placed the casket atop a stack of padlocked chests.

"Is there aught else I can do for you?"

"You could give me your guess as to what this is worth."

She withdrew the folded handkerchief from her pocket and unwrapped the cloth to reveal a small ruby. Its shape was irregular, as most gems' were, but its color was a deep and fiery red.

"That looks to be a fine stone," Sir Hugh commented.

"It is." She passed it to him so he could hold it to the light. "From an island to the east of the Levant, I'm told."

"How did you come by it, if I may ask?"

"It was a gift from the sultan of J'bara. He gave it to me after my father took the arrow intended for him. My sire had sold his sword in service to the sultan, you see, and…"

"The devil you say! Simon de Brac was in service to an infidel?"

Hastily, Eleanor tried to explain the Byzantine maze of alliances that pitted tribe against tribe and desert sheik against sheik.

"The sultan of J'bara holds the oasis of Dazur, a vital stopping point on the trade route that cuts through territory held by the Emir of Damascus. But he hates the emir for beheading his brother, and since the emir is allied with Saladin in his war with the Christian kings, J'bara fights with us."

"The enemy of my enemy is my friend," Hugh said dryly. "It's the same here in England. Only now, with King Henry dead and many arguing whether Richard or Arthur should wear his crown, it grows more difficult by the day to know which is which."

He rolled the ruby between his fingers, testing its weight while he admired its color. "So Simon de Brac took an arrow meant for this sultan and you received this in recompense."

"Aye."

That, and the other items in the casket Eleanor had just given Exmoor for safekeeping. She started to tell him of those but the flash of fear she'd seen in Catherine's eyes held her back.

She didn't know this man. The bits of information she'd gleaned from Sir Giles suggested he was a fair and honorable overlord. But Giles was his vassal. He would hardly say otherwise. Especially to a woman he was delivering into the man's care. She'd wait, Eleanor decided, and take the lord of Exmoor's measure a little more before entrusting him with her true circumstances.

"I know the stone's value in the East," she said, "but am not sure what it would fetch here."

Hugh eyed the ruby again. It was small and shaped by natural forces but the color shone dark and fine. He had a good notion of what the gem would bring, but wanted to know first why Eleanor wanted to part with it.

"What do you wish to buy with this?"

"A palfrey for Jasmine and a mount trained to the hunt for me," she replied promptly. "Stout boots and shoes for us both. Silks for embroidering. And cloth to make new gowns." Her lips tilted. "Our robes, as you must see, are sadly outmoded."

He returned the ruby to her hand. "Keep your stone. I have suitable mounts for you and your sister in my stables. The tanner will cut your shoes and boots, and my lady mother will supply what cloth and silks you need."

"I thank you, sir, but that will not do."

Hugh blinked. A lord's word was law here in the Western Marches, where the palatine barons ruled with far more freedoms than those in the rest of England. Few men would dare to say him nay. That this slender, flame-haired slip of a girl would do so, and in such a firm tone, was not to his liking.

"Your pardon, lady?"

That cool reply would have made any of his vassals blanch and take a quick step back. All it wrought from Eleanor de Brac was a brisk apology.

"Forgive me. I don't wish to sound ungrateful. But neither do I wish to be a charge on you or Lady Alice."

"As long as you and your sister are in my care, I will provide for your needs."

She opened her mouth to protest. Hugh forestalled her by reaching out and folding her fingers around the stone.

"Enough, lady. Save your bauble to buy presents at Christmastide. Or to use as dower, should you take a husband."

Her gaze dropped to his fist, wrapped around hers. So did his. Struck by the warmth and warmth of her skin, Hugh dropped his hand.

"I do indeed wish to take a husband," she told him. "It's why I've come to England."

He lifted a brow. "Were there none to be had in Outremer?"

"Oh, aye. I had offers enough. None that my sire deemed worthy, however." A twinkle lit her green eyes. "They were too much like him, you see. Ragtag knights and mercenaries come to the Levant to make their fortunes, and I had no dower to bring them until my father took that arrow. Then there was Jasmine." The laughter left her eyes. "Although alliances are tangled, as I've said, the battle scars between the Franks and Saracens run long and deep. Her mother was a slave. A woman of the desert won by my father on a roll of the dice. So…So I thought it best to remove her from danger whilst I could."

"You're a most loyal sister."

"She's all I have."

"Until you take a husband."

"Until I take a husband," she agreed. "And I would ask your advice in that matter once Jasmine and I have found our feet. But I do not wish be a burden to you betimes. So I must insist you take this ruby and…"

"Enough, I say." The warning was flat and unmistakable this time. "I have given you the shelter of my house and my name. That's all you need until you go to your husband."

Her mouth clamped shut. Temper flared in her green eyes. Hugh waited, wondering if she would dare loose it.

Wisely, she did not. She swallowed her ire, but from the look on her face, it left a bitter taste. Her chin tilting, she regarded him with something less than friendliness.

"Are you always this proud and overbearing, sir?"

"Aye. Are you always this stubborn and disrespectful?"

"Aye." Her temper faded, to be replaced by a reluctant smile. "You can't imagine how many hours I've spent on my knees or how many *pater nosters* I've said in hopes God would help me curb my strong will."

Quite the contrary. Hugh could well imagine it. "I'm surprised your father did not cut a stout switch and curb it for you."

She heaved a long sigh. "It pains me to say so, sir, but my father was wont to scurry out the back door when he heard me come in the front. He had grown used to me managing his affairs, you see, and preferred not to be troubled by trifling matters that could upon occasion upset me."

Like unpaid shield makers, importuning farriers and irate wine sellers. Eleanor had learned to deal with every sort of merchant and moneylender, which was why it did not sit well with her now to become beholden to Exmoor.

She could tell by the set to his chin that this was not the time to argue the matter, however. He wore his austere, lord of the manner air again. And to tell the truth, that flat dictate some moments ago had raised the hairs on the back of her neck. Hugh Montmercy could be rather intimidating when he chose.

She began to understand Lady Catherine's nervousness. The girl's life would be miserable indeed if she could not conquer her fears and learn to deal with her lord.

It did Eleanor not one whit of good to remind herself that Catherine's problem was not hers, that few women could boast the freedoms she herself had enjoyed at the hands of her ramshackle sire. Nor did she know what bits of advice she could offer the girl. It was obvious Catherine's estate was far above hers. Moreover, the girl had lived in Exmoor's shadow for two years. Surely she must know his ways by now.

She would watch, Eleanor decided. Listen. Take the man's measure, as she'd already determined to do. Between helping Catherine come to grip with her fears, keeping a rein on Jasmine's high spirits, and finding a husband for herself, she looked to have her hands full.

And here she'd worried that she would not find sufficient outlet for her energies without a household of her own to manage!

Much cheered by the knowledge she'd have some challenging tasks to keep her busy, she accepted the arm Exmoor offered and accompanied him abovestairs to dinner.

Chapter Three

The meal turned out to be a lively occasion. Knights in service to Exmoor crowded the boards, some with their ladies, others elbow-to-elbow while they shared a trencher. A small army of servants, squires and pages ferried food, ale and wine. Unmarried girls, widows, and other females were seated according to the rank and marital status. And everyone, it seemed, was eager to hear about events in the East.

To Eleanor's surprise, Sir Hugh raised her above her station and placed her at the high table beside the doughty Sir Giles and his wife. Lady Alice sat on her son's left, and Catherine held the place of honor on his right. The girl seemed to take little pride in her high position, though. Silent as a wraith, she left the ordering of the servants and pages to Lady Alice.

The boards groaned with the weight of summer bounty. Game birds swam in rich sauces. Venison stewed in onions and wild mushrooms vied for space with a roasted boar still sporting its tusks. Plump lingonberries added both color and tartness to mutton steaks. Sir Giles speared a piece of sugared mackerel and placed it on his wife's trencher before turning to Eleanor.

"Does Conrad of Montferrat still hold Tyre against the Saracens?" he asked as he performed the same courtesy for her.

"Indeed he does, Sir. Or did when Jasmine and I set sail some months ago."

As she cut into her own portion of mackerel with her eating knife, Eleanor kept a wary eye on her sister, seated between two girls in wardship to Exmoor.

"Tyre is the last great fortress to hold out against the Saracens," she related between dainty bites. "Saladin besieged it twice, but could not take it as he did Antioch, Acre, Sidon, and Jerusalem."

A rumble went around the boards at her mention of the holiest of cities. Like all good Christians, the men and women of Exmoor were outraged by its capture. They peppered Eleanor with questions about the siege and subsequent flight the king of Jerusalem.

"We shall reclaim what was lost," Sir Giles vowed grimly. "All the kings of Europe have answered the Pope's call and taken the Cross. Frederick Barbarossa has already assembled a vast army and begun his march to Constantinople. Phillip of France is ready to take ship with his. Sancho of Navarre is too busy fighting the Moors in Spain to go himself, but sends men and arms."

"And Richard Lionheart, who was the first to sew a red cross to his tunic, now frets to join the rest." Sir Giles' wife added with a quick glance at her husband. "The whole world, it seems, has taken up arms, or soon will."

"Except those barons Richard bid stay and hold his lands for him," Lady Alice put in, eyeing her son with the same worried look. "The Church has promised them forgiveness for not going on Crusade if they will send monies or men."

Eleanor could understand the women's reluctance to see their menfolk depart for this, the third great Crusade. Many of those who'd answered the call for the first two had never returned. Thousands of Frankish knights were now buried far from home. Others, mostly landless mercenaries like her father, had chosen to remain in the East in hopes of plunder.

Curious as to whether Exmoor would take the Cross, Eleanor slanted him a glance. Whatever his intent, he kept it to himself. His face gave no clue to his thoughts as he cut a choice morsel of boar for his betrothed.

"And pay they do," Sir Giles muttered in response to Lady Alice's remark. "That damned Saladin Tithe. Small wonder the barons grow so restive."

"The English barons pay tithe to Prince Saladin?" Eleanor asked in surprise. "Do they think to ransom all the knights he has taken prisoner?"

"No, lady! They think to defeat him! Before he died, King Henry ordered every man in England, from the lowest peasant to the greatest lord, to give one-tenth of his rents and moveable goods to help retake Jerusalem. The monies are even now being collected in the presence of a parish priest, a Knight Templar, a servant of the King, and the clerk of the bishop. Any who does not pay his rightful share will be excommunicated."

"And the barons grow restive over this?"

"Some do."

"Because it is over and above what they already owe their liege in rents and service?"

"Because the monies go into the king's coffers," Sir Giles replied, scowling, "and not those of the Church. It's a not a tithe at all, but a tax that wears the guise of one."

Eleanor wasn't sure she saw the difference, but Exmoor stilled his vassal with a small shake of his head and turned the conversation. "Such weighty matters are better left to the council chamber than the great hall. Rather we should entertain our guests. Catherine, what would you have the minstrels sing?"

"Wh... Whatever you wish, my lord."

"Come, sweeting, there must be a song *you* would wish to hear."

"I...uh..." The girl slicked her tongue nervously over her lips. "I would hear a ballad."

Nodding, Exmoor signaled to the minstrels roving the hall. Their leader, a stout fellow with bells tinkling at the end of his long cap, took his order and immediately piped a tune on his flute. The boy who accompanied him on the mandolin began to sing of Chyld Wynn and the beauteous Lady Margaret.

Both music and conversation continued through the stuffed quarter of bear, salted walnuts, salmon in orange sauce, squirrel stew, and cakes with honey. Once the scraps were gathered to give to the beggars and the bones fed to the dogs, the servants removed the boards and the minstrels struck up roundel.

Eleanor's toe tapped in time to the music. She would have accepted Sir Giles' polite offer to lead her in dance, but the sight of Jasmine's slumped shoulders and mulish mouth changed her mind. The girl was difficult enough to manage when she was in high spirits. Tired and ill-humored, she could test the fortitude of a saint. Pleading weariness from her long journey, Eleanor thanked Lady Alice and her son for their warm welcome and took her sister to bed.

Hugh watched her weave her way through the dancers, as did many of the other men in the hall. Her outmoded robe and veil did little to hide the vibrant woman beneath the layers.

"Hugh."

His mother's soft voice wrenched his gaze from the slender back and hips girded by a braided belt. "You should partner your lady."

"And so I should," he agreed, turning to the girl at his side. "Will you take my hand, Catherine, if I promise not to tread upon your feet?"

Her reply was a mere whisper. "If you wish, my lord."

Swallowing an oath, Hugh took her hand, but led her to a quiet corner instead of to the floor.

"You... You do not wish to dance after all?" she asked.

"I do, but I would speak with you first." He drew a breath, knowing he was about to tread on thin ice but felt compelled to address her barely veiled fears. "I know our marriage isn't to your liking, Catherine. Do you but say the word, and I will I speak to your father. Mayhap we could find a way to nullify our vows."

"No!" Panic sprang into her eyes. Her nails dug furrows in his hand. "No, I beg you!"

Hugh smothered another oath. Catherine lived in greater terror of her father than she did of him. And with good reason. Her sire had bedded, bruised, and buried three wives. He'd also sold his bevy of daughters to the highest bidders without regard for their welfare or desire. His cruelty to the women in his household was the reason Hugh had insisted his young bride reside with him until she was of an age - and of a mind - to be bedded.

Jesu, but that state was slow in coming!

Her father's brutality to his wives had imbued Catherine with a deep-seated terror of the marriage bed. Hugh had wooed her gently these past two years and done his best to ease that fear. For her part, his mother had spoken frankly of the pleasures to be found in the marriage bed. As had, he'd been told, a number of young wives closer to Catherine's age. To no avail. The scars his betrothed carried from witnessing the vicious way her mother and step-mothers had been used were etched deep on her soul. So deep the girl spent many an hour in the chapel every day, praying for the strength to overcome them. Too many hours, in truth.

Even as Hugh acknowledged how deep his wife's scars ran, a familiar frustration came near to strangling him. It wasn't that he ached to pierce her maiden shield. His appetites were strong but did not run to forcing her or any other woman. He could take his ease on many a willing serving wench, merchant's wife, or light-skirted lady.

Time pressed in on him, however. Despite Catherine's fear, he couldn't delay bedding her much longer. Richard would soon arrive in England to take the crown. When he did, he'd look for ways to wring even more monies from his barons for his Crusade. He could well decide to double or triple the bride price Hugh must pay the crown when he and Catherine formalized their marriage.

Or Richard might sell her to someone who would pay even more. Kings had ways to nullify even the most sacred vows when they proved inconvenient. As did queens. Richard's mother, Eleanor, had obtained an annulment to set aside her fifteen year union with Louis of France so she could marry the lusty young Henry Plantagenet. And now Richard himself sought to end his betrothal to Alys of France, who was rumored to have become mistress to his father.

"Please, my lord," Catherine begged, dragging Hugh's thoughts from Richard Lionheart's tangled affairs to his own. "Do not send me back to my father!"

Hugh couldn't help but contrast this frightened maid with the flame-haired woman who'd stood toe to toe with him in the counting room a short time ago. Would that Catherine possessed even a small measure of Eleanor de Brac's spirit and fire.

Thrusting aside the disloyal thought, he bent to brush a kiss across his promised wife's trembling mouth. "No, sweeting, I will not send you back to your father."

Chapter Four

From the little Eleanor had told him of her life in the East, Hugh suspected that she and her sister might need some time to adjust to life at Exmoor. Still, he was surprised when the keep's priest sent a note not two days later begging for a few moments of his time to discuss a concern regarding the Lady Eleanor.

Father Anselem was a gentle soul, a learned scholar and the spiritual leader of the two other priests who served the parish. In addition to performing Mass, he often assisted Hugh by acting as witness on legal documents and Lady Alice by reading to her and her ladies from sacred texts. It was unusual for this kindly, gray-haired priest to voice even the smallest criticism, so Hugh went at once to the chantry and knelt for Father Anselem's blessing. The elderly priest gave it and gestured to a book bound in red leather lying open on his table.

"I'm most reluctant to bring this to your attention, my son, but felt I must."

He passed the book to Hugh, who frowned at the strange black markings on its cover. "What is this?"

"A collection of tales from the East, according to the Lady Eleanor. Heretical stories of flying carpets and grand viziers and jiniis that spring from brass lamps. She's been reading them to your mother and her ladies."

Startled, Hugh glanced again at the indecipherable squiggles. That Eleanor had been taught to read was surprise enough given what she'd let drop about her sire and her unconventional upbringing. That she could read what he now guessed was Arabic surprised him even more.

"She was most obliging when I asked to see the book," Father Anselem related. "And when I ventured to suggest the stories might not be suitable for the delicate ears of your lady wife and the other maidens in your keeping, she did not argue."

"So I would hope."

"I don't think I convinced her imp of a sister, however. Mistress Jasmine preceded to inform me that the people of the desert fly through the air on carpets all the time." A wry smile tugged at the priest's lips. "Jasmine seems to have convinced your brother of that. I can only pray Master Guy doesn't attempt to launch himself from one of the upper windows."

Hugh could visualize such an attempt all too clearly! "I'll speak to Guy. Is he at his lessons with Father Guillaume?"

"Well… Ah…"

The kindly priest was clearly loath to bring the older brother's wrath down on the younger. Hugh shook his head, caught between the familiar combination of amused affection and exasperation that his scamp of a brother often stirred in him.

"He's playing the slacker again, is he? Never mind. I suspect I know where to find him."

Guy wasn't at the stables, however, or the kennels. When Hugh tried the kitchens, another of the lad's favorite hide-aways, the spit-turner basting a haunch of venison pointed his wooden ladle at a window with a view of the orchard.

Hugh heard the shrieks of laughter well before he entered the orchard and spotted his errant brother. Shaded by a flowering pear tree, Guy was strutting like a peacock. He'd swathed his head in a shawl to form a turban. A sash of some shimmering material circled his waist. His overlarge feet, Hugh saw, were half in and half out of curly toed slippers that obviously belonged to the barefoot girl perched on a low hanging limb.

But it was the third member of the trio that riveted Hugh's gaze. She sat cross-legged on the grass, leaning back on her hands, her skirts pooled around her and a circlet of dandelions anchoring her veil. Her face was alight with laughter as her young sister encouraged Guy in his antics.

"Now wrinkle your nose," Jasmine ordered from her tree branch, swinging her bare feet. "And walk as if you've stepped in offal. There! Now you look much like the fat turd who wanted to add Eleanor to his harem."

"His harem?" Guy stopped in mid-prance and looked at Eleanor with wide eyes. "Really?"

Hugh paused behind a screen of leafy branches, as interested as his brother in her answer.

"I thanked the sultan very prettily," she related, grinning, "but told him I would fain return to the land of my father. S'truth, I could not see myself draped in veils, lolling about on cushions and stuffing myself with sweetmeats with his other wives and concubines."

Hugh had no such problem. An image leaped instantly in his head of Eleanor de Brac draped in the sheerest of veils and curled seductively on embroidered cushions. With her lean, lithe body and flame-bright hair, the woman would make a thoroughly seductive odalisque.

The all-too-vivid picture hit like a mailed fist. His belly clenched, fast and tight, as he stared at this laughing creature crowned with dandelions. He ached to crush that ripe, smiling mouth under his. To send the youngsters away, stretch her out on the grass, and...

Sweet Jesu! He was betrothed to Catherine. Will she or nil she, the timid young maid would soon be his wife in fact as well as in name. Hugh was a cur of the lowest sort to lust for another woman in the same household. But lust he did, and the realization disgusted him. Swallowing an oath, he strode through the gnarled trees to make his presence known.

"You've most entertaining tales of the East, lady." He turned a minatory eye on Guy. "And you, brother, are supposed to be at your lessons."

The lad quailed but gamely stood his ground. "I am at lessons, Hugh. Lady Eleanor has been teaching me to count in the way of the East, with Arabic numbers instead of Roman numerals."

"Has she?"

"But look." His turban slipped as he bent and snatched up a piece of parchment filled with charcoal markings. "There are ten numbers," he explained eagerly as he righted his ridiculous headdress. "You can double and triple them most readily. It makes deciphering so much easier."

The numbers intrigued Hugh. He would've asked Guy's instructress to explain the system if not for the need to quash any desire his brother might harbor to fly.

"I hear you've also been learning tales of genies and magic carpets."

"Oh, dear," Eleanor murmured. "You've gotten word of that, have you?"

When she gathered her skirts and started to rise, Hugh reached down to aid her. Her skin was soft and warm, her grip surprisingly strong. She gained her feet and showed a rueful face under her crown of dandelions.

"Father Anselem hinted that the tales might not be suitable for your ladies but I thought them safe for such an adventurous, inquisitive lad as your brother."

"Therein lies the problem, lady. After hearing these tales, he's like as not to try sailing out of a window on a carpet."

"Surely not!"

Only when she started to turn toward the boy did Hugh realize he still gripped her hand in his. She flashed a quick glance at their joined hands, then lifted those mesmerizing emerald eyes until he released her.

"Tell me you would never do anything so foolish, Guy."

The lad's expression was answer enough. He remained silent but Jasmine showed no such restraint. Dropping from her perch on the low-hanging tree branch, she stood faced Hugh with utter fearlessness.

"The tales are true! The people of the desert know many incantations and magic spells."

"Mayhap they do," he replied coolly. "You, however, are not in the desert. Such spells and incantations would not work here."

Uncertainty chased across her young face. Frowning, she looked to her sister, and Eleanor hastened to add her warning to Hugh's.

"That's true, Jasmine. This is a different clime altogether, with different tales and legends. Perhaps Guy would deign to share them with you?"

"What do I care of tales with no genies or dragons?"

"We have woodland fairies," her faithful young swain put in helpfully.

"Pah!"

"And dragons and griffins."

The girl flapped a hand and stalked off. Obviously affronted by her abrupt dismissal of anything not pertaining to the desert, Guy kicked out of her slippers and followed.

"It appears your sister has made a conquest," Hugh observed drily as his brother hurried after the stiff shouldered girl.

"So it does. Would that his merry spirit will lift hers," Eleanor added with a sigh. "Jasmine has yet to accustom herself to the ways of the West. I fear she finds them most restrictive."

"And you, lady? Do you also find them restrictive?"

"I must confess that I do. I'm more used to haggling in the bazar and struggling with my father's accounts than embroidering altar cloths. Oh, your lady mother has been most kind," she added hastily when Hugh frowned. "She's set her ladies to sewing new gowns for Jasmine and me and had the tanner make us new boots. Quite elegant ones, don't you think?"

She lifted her skirt to display a dainty foot shod in supple leather dyed a bright azure.

"Very elegant," Hugh agreed as his gaze roamed from the ankle boot to the smooth, curved length of stockinged calf above it. The visceral impact of that shapely limb disturbed him almost as much as the careless way she displayed it.

"Life here must indeed be a change for both you and your sister," he said, more brusquely than he intended. "I would prefer you assist in the sewing of your new robes, however, rather than encourage Guy to play the truant."

The smile left her eyes. She dropped her skirts and dipped her head in a cool nod. "As you wish, m'lord."

Hugh could only hope his warning had taken root. He discovered his mistake not three days later.

He'd ridden out to inspect an outlying demesne and returned to find the ladies of Exmoor gathered in the garden. Drawn by their merry laughter, he passed his helm and gauntlets to his squire, pushed back his mailed hood, and crossed to the garden gate.

He wasn't the only one drawn there, he saw. Edward Arrowshanks, his chief fletcher, stood by with well-filled quivers. His brother Guy was there, too, the boy's head topped by the turban he appeared to have adopted as his own. Gathered around him were a number of other squires and pages who should have been about their tasks. Frowning, Hugh noted several of his men-at-arms had drifted from their posts on the curtain wall to watch the women.

Or, rather, to watch the woman who stood at the mark, notching an arrow to her bowstring. With her face alight and her fiery hair escaping from her veil and circlet, she caught every eye. The new bliaut she'd sewn for herself was laced tight across her breasts in the current style. An embroidered girdle encircled her slender waist and drew Hugh's gaze to the swell of hip below.

His jaw went tight as a now-familiar combination of desire and self-disgust curled in his belly. Eleanor de Brac was all that he admired, all he desired, in a woman. Merry of temperament. Supple of body. As learned as any of the ladies who'd traveled to the Levant with

Queen Eleanor on the Second Crusade so many years ago. And, apparently, well skilled in archery.

"I cannot shoot as far as you, with your longer English bows," she said, her voice carrying clearly on the hot, still air, "but mayhap I can shoot faster."

Taking aim at the straw target, she loosed the arrow. Almost before it hit, she plucked another from the three stuck in the ground before her, notched it, and let fly. Her speed was blinding, her eye unerring. One after the other, her arrows hit the target center.

"Well done, lady!"

The booming accolade came from the brawny young knight who stepped out of the shadows of the keep. The man had served as Hugh's squire until he won his spurs two years ago. He was now a captain of the guard. And should, like his men-at-arms, be about his duties instead of gawking like the veriest straw-head, Hugh thought sourly.

"Only tell me," the knight asked, "do the Saracens piss upon their arrow points to cause wounds to fester, as our archers do?"

The other ladies frowned at his frank speaking but Eleanor had lived too long amid war to dismiss the question lightly. "Aye, they do. I have not witnessed the practice myself, you understand, but have seen the fetid and festering wounds such poisoned arrows cause."

"What of their war hammers?" another knight wanted to know. "I'm told they're fitted with a curved spike that's as deadly on the backswing as the club is on the fore."

"Our father had such a war club," Jasmine put in. "He smashed many a skull with it."

Eleanor turned to smile at her and only then saw the girl had taken up the bow and notched an arrow. "Jasmine! Do not!"

Her cry came too late. The girl had already loosed the string. Because her arms were so much shorter and her strength less, she'd drawn it only halfway. As a consequence, the arrow wobbled rather than flew and took a dangerous turn. When it plowed into the dirt a mere three inches from Guy's feet, the lad thought it a great joke.

Hugh did not. The damned shaft might have hit any of those present, including Catherine or Eleanor herself. Striding forward, he yanked the bow from the younger sister's hand and thrust it at the elder.

"I would that you have more care with this, and with your charge."

Eleanor cast the girl a fulminating look. "I will endeavor to do so, my lord."

"You'd best do more than endeavor."

He hadn't intended to sound so short. Nor would he, if he hadn't been distracted by the perspiration that gave her face a warm sheen and set the loose tendrils of her hair to curling wildly.

Eleanor stiffened at his tone. Her exasperation faded, as did the warmth in her cheeks. "She's but a child, sir."

Guy, too, was moved to champion his friend. Righting the turban that had slipped down to cover his right eye, he offered a dubious defense. "Jasmine is better with her dagger than the bow, brother. Truly."

To Hugh's surprise, even Catherine overcame her bone-deep shyness to lay an arm across Jasmine's shoulders. "She meant no harm."

The lord of Exmoor knew when to stand his ground and when to beat a strategic retreat. Faced with such a solid front, he adopted the even tone he always used with his betrothed. "I know she meant no harm."

The tone he employed with Eleanor was considerably less temperate. "Just have an eye to her."

As he strode away, Eleanor's breath left on an irritated huff. Twice now Exmoor had chastised her. She didn't like it any better this time than the last. Rounding on her sister, she struggled to rein in her temper.

"Go to the women's bower, untangle your sewing silks and work on the altar cloth. I'll be up to inspect your stitches in a little while."

The girl opened her mouth, ready as ever with a fervent argument.

"Now, Jasmine!"

"Pah!"

Eleanor's temper simmered just under her skin as she gathered her bow and unused arrows. The other ladies drifted away, but the kind-hearted Catherine came to assist her.

"I begin to see why you hold Sir Hugh in such dislike," Eleanor muttered.

"Oh, no!" The younger woman's face turned pale above the cornflower blue of her gown. "You mistake the matter. I do not dislike him. How could I, when he is always so kind to me?"

Exasperated, Eleanor flopped onto a nearby bench. "Forgive me. You do not dislike him, you merely live in terror of him."

"Aye," the girl whispered raggedly. "I do."

In truth, Eleanor could fathom neither Exmoor nor his promised wife. She'd witnessed his small kindnesses and unfailing courtesy toward his betrothed, yet the girl all but trembled every time he came near her.

"Why do you fear him, if he's so kind to you?"

"Because...."

"Because?"

Red suffused the heart-shaped face that had been so pale a moment ago. "He would use me. As...as..."

Eleanor made a wild guess. "As a man uses a woman?"

"As a boar does a sow!" the girl burst out. "Or a stallion covering a mare!"

"But you're to be his wife!. Of course he'll mate with you. Mayhap not like a boar or a stallion but…"

"I fear it," Catherine burst out, her voice tortured. "However it's done, I cannot sleep for fearing it."

Eleanor's heart twisted with pity for the terrified young maid. She herself had yet to surrender her virginity, but she'd lived long enough in the East to hear the most lurid and deliciously tantalizing tales of the harem. She'd also been given some very frank advice from the women who occasionally shared her father's bed and board.

"Oh, Catherine! Surely Lady Alice or the other women have told you there are ways to make the breaching easier."

"Aye, they have." Head hanging, she pleated the folds of her gown. "And I know Hugh will have a care of me. But…"

A shudder ripped through her. When she lifted her head, her face was as white as a shroud. "But I heard the screams when my father bedded his last wife. It took two men to hold her down while he had her."

"God's bones!"

"My father was most displeased with her screeching. She wore the marks of his fist for a month."

"You must know Sir Hugh would never use you so."

"I do! I swear I do! I have prayed and prayed for the courage to do my duty, but I cannot rid my head of those screams."

"Does Hugh know the reason for your fears?"

"Aye," she whispered.

A bee buzzed about Eleanor's ear. Distracted, she flapped a hand and shooed it away. "Let me think on this," she said after a moment. "There must be something I can do."

"You?" Startled, Catherine stammered an apology. "Your pardon, Eleanor. I should *not* have burdened you with my foolish frights. Please, you mustn't trouble yourself over it."

"Of course I must. I'm your aunt of sorts, am I not?"

The girl looked doubtful but was too polite to argue the matter.

"Let me think on this," Eleanor said again. "You and Sir Hugh have not yet fixed on a date to repeat your vows *verba de praesenti*, have you?"

"No."

"Then we have time yet to put our heads together," she said with cheerful reassurance. "Between us, we will find a way to chivvy you from your fear of the marriage bed."

As it turned out, Eleanor had little time to think on Catherine's problem. The very next afternoon, a courier arrived with word that Richard Lionheart would take ship for England within the month.

The news spurred a flurry of sewing and stitching of new gowns in the ladies' bower, and much gossip about the handsome, as-yet unwed and uncrowned king. It also spurred a summons for Hugh to meet with the other barons of the western Marches. That in turn spawned far greater problems than any Eleanor could have anticipated.

Chapter Five

The July morning was hot and dry when Hugh rode out at the head of a small troop to answer the Earl of Chester's summons. He took with him only his squire, young Thomas Beckwith, and ten mounted men-at-arms. They made good progress until they had to stop to deal with a band of thieves who'd attacked a hapless merchant and his escort. As a consequence, Hugh arrived at the ancient city that served as the earl's seat later in the afternoon than he'd anticipated.

Founded by the Romans, Chester had changed hands many times over the centuries. It had been held first by the Welsh, then by Saxons, Danes and the Welsh again. Guy d'Avranches conquered it in the name of King Edgar and constructed a mighty castle atop the mound that had once been a Saxon stronghold. Hugh knew a pang of envy mixed with admiration for the castle's massive size and formidable battlements as he and his troop approached it.

The captain of the guard recognized the Exmoor eagle and sent word of his arrival. To Hugh's delight, the knight who strode out of the keep to greet him was not his liege lord, the Earl of Chester, but William, known to all by his family's hereditary title as The Marshal.

Signaling to his squire to hold his stirrup, Hugh hastily dismounted and braced himself for the blow he knew would come. "My lord Marshal."

"Exmoor, you young dog. It's about time you showed your face."

A fist as hard and unforgiving as a stone shot from a catapult plowed into Hugh's shoulder. Not for William Marshal the genteel kiss of peace most lords exchanged. He could curb neither his strength nor his bluff, hearty manner.

Hugh had served as squire to the Marshal and knew him to be as stout of heart as he was true to his honor. The younger son of a minor knight, Marshal had amassed lands and ransoms and a fearsome reputation in tournaments. Rumor was he'd bested more than five hundred knights in tourneys. Having fought alongside him on the field of battle, Hugh didn't doubt the number.

Like most of the Marcher lords, Marshal was also caught in a web of tangled loyalties. As a young knight, he'd won the admiration of Queen Eleanor with his prowess on the field and his courtly manner off of it. King Henry, also impressed, had appointed him tutor to his heir, Young King Hal. When Hal died and the next in line to the crown, Richard Lionheart, revolted against his father to gain more autonomy, William Marshal remained loyal to Henry. He had even at one point unhorsed Richard on the field of battle, the only warrior rumored to have ever done so.

In gratitude for Marshal's help in subduing his son's revolt, Henry promised him the hand and vast estates of Isabel de Clare, to include the earldom of Pembroke. Now Henry was dead and the prince William had battled against was coming to claim his throne. The Marshal must be wondering whether Richard would hold to his father's promises.

He was also, Hugh discovered, wondering where his former squire had acquired his current mount. Eyes gleaming, the Marshal skimmed an admiring glance from Sirocco's fine-boned head to his flanks.

"How did you come by this magnificent animal?"

"He was a gift."

"Would that someone should gift me with such a steed!"

Much as Hugh loved the Marshal, he was not about to take the hint. Instead, he signaled to Thomas to take Sirocco's reins and crossed the bailey with his former lord.

"What news of Richard?" he asked as they mounted the steps to the keep. "When does he arrive in England?"

"Within the month, we're told. Until then, he leaves all matters here in his mother's hands." The Marshal shook his head in admiration for a woman he'd once wooed with no hope of ever winning her. "She's as much a great lady - and busy queen - as ever."

That was certainly the truth. In the short weeks since she emerged from her long imprisonment, Eleanor had issued numerous edits in her son's name. Her first act, in fact, had been to order the release of large numbers of felons who'd committed crimes such as poaching or slanderizing. As she was said to remark when signing the writ, she knew firsthand how odious prisons were to both men and women.

In a subsequent wave of reforms, she standardized weights and measures for cloth and wheat throughout the realm. Even more significant, she set a single value for coinage to end regional differences. While the Marcher lords were not yet decided as to the efficacy of that, all agreed that the previous fluctuations in the price of silver had benefitted primarily bankers and moneylenders. Still, even those reforms did not alleviate the widespread dissatisfaction with the Saladin tax.

The most pressing concern at present, however, was the missive sent to all great lords and prelates, summoning them to London at a date to be specified to *bear fealty to the lord Richard, lord of England and son the the lord king Henry and the lady Eleanor, in life and limb and earthly honor, as liege lord.*

"Will you go?" Hugh asked William

"I lean in that direction, but many others have yet to decide their course." The old warrior smiled wryly. "Eleanor's offering the enticement of a great tourney to draw in the knights."

"She's rescinded Henry's ban?"

"She has, in Richard's name."

The news didn't surprise Hugh. Tournaments had long provided knights a valuable source of income in ransoms paid by knights bested on the tourney field. But Henry had banned the war games in England for fear that his too-often rebellious lords would summon heavily armed knights to tourney, then use their massed strength to challenge his sovereignty. His sons, however, had regularly competed in tourneys on the Continent. So it came as no surprise that Richard would instruct his mother to re-institute the games in England, particularly since anyone desiring to host such an event would pay a stiff license fee to the crown.

Hugh tucked the information away for further consideration as he and the Marshal joined the other barons gathered for council in Chester's great hall. As befitting his rank, Marshal resumed his seat at the high table with the earls of Chester, Hereford, and Shrewsbury.

These great Marcher lords owed allegiance to the English king in times of war. As reward for holding the western borders against the pesky Welsh, however, they exercised considerable independence. Most considered themselves a law unto themselves. They could create markets and boroughs and forest preserves as they saw fit. They also appointed their own justicars and paid no royal taxes…except the Saladin tax, which had them all grumbling. Even more worrisome, though, was the very real possibility that Richard Lionheart might avenge old wrongs by stripping them of their lands and titles.

As a consequence, several objected when William Marshall recommended against immediate action and suggested they not take up arms against Richard until they saw which way the wind blew.

"Why wait until he's gained his crown and we must go against an anointed king?" Guy de Kevelioc countered. The fifth to carry the title of Earl of Chester, he was Hugh's liege lord for the holding of Exmoor.

"What matter a few sprinkles of holy water?" the Marshal retorted. "I don't need to remind you that many here have raised arms against anointed kings before."

"With a rich prize like Isabel de Clare dangling before your nose, I would think you'd be the first to lead the charge."

Marshal stiffened and flashed the earl a look of pure contempt. "Some of us value honor above riches, de Kevelioc."

The Earl of Hereford intervened with a hasty request to hear the opinions of the assembled vassals. When a baron near doubled over with age began a long-winded discourse about how Richard's eagerness to leave on Crusade might work to the benefit on them all, the lord seated next to Hugh gave a divisive snort.

"Marshal speaks of honor," he muttered. "But for a man of forty and more years, he was quick enough snap up the offer of tender young Isabel. If she has yet to see her fifteenth name day, I'll eat my hauberk."

Hugh slanted the man a cool glance. He had little liking for John Powrys, Baron Penhammond. The man was dark of hair and eye, with the lean cheeks and the same hungry look as the black wolf that decorated his surcoat.

"As best I recall, Penhammond, you owe vassalage to the Marshal."

"You recall correctly. And if memory serves *me*, Exmoor, you are betrothed to Catherine of

Langmont. Not as rich a wife as Isabel de Clare, but a plump little pigeon nonetheless. You'd best hope Richard does not convince her father to give the girl to someone willing to pay a more exorbitant bride price."

Hugh didn't bother to answer, although he could see behind the baron's sneer easily enough. The Saladin tax had strapped him, as it had so many barons who lived by their rents and their wits. Hugh guessed Penhammond vacillated between rising against Richard in hopes of claiming a wealthy heiress as a prize or throwing in with the new king to the same end.

All too well aware that the weeks ahead were fraught with danger, Hugh turned his attention back to the high table.

He left Chester the following morning. Arguments for and against swearing allegiance to Richard had lasted late into the night, with the Marshal finally convincing all to wait until they had a better grasp of the new king's intentions.

As Hugh and his troop followed the broad banks of the River Dee, he acknowledged to himself that he'd needed no such convincing. His allegiance lay with the crown. Although he owed vassalage to the Earl of Chester for Exmoor, he owed the same to Richard for Bellemeade and his estates in Normandy and Anjou. None none of those properties were as rich as Exmoor, to be sure, but their roots went back several centuries. If it came to open rebellion, Hugh would stand with Richard.

Consumed by his thoughts, he greeted with relief the distant silhouette of Exmoor keep standing strong atop its earthen mound. For now at least, he could tend to his own affairs while Richard tended to his.

The relief lasted only until he spotted what looked like a pillar of smoke snaking up against a backdrop of gray, scudding clouds. His heart leaped into his throat when he saw the smoke came from Exmoor's outer bailey.

"With me!"

He put his spurs to Sirocco. The courser leaped forward, then flew like the desert wind he was named for. With each thud of hooves against the beaten earth track, Hugh leaned low across his neck and assessed the situation.

The gate to the bailey stood open. The bridge across the moat was lowered. There was no sign of attack. No siege engines, no enemy pennants flying in the discernible distance. Villeins still hoed the fields. Pigs and chickens rooted in the dirt in the village.

Yet as he and his troop thundered up the sloping hill to the keep, he could hear cries and shouts. And when he drew reign in the outer bailey, his chest heaving and his heart slamming against his ribs, he found it a scene of utter chaos.

His thunderous arrival cut through the tumult. The crowd in the outer yard seemed to turn as one, their faces showing every emotion from surprise to relief to fear. Drawing rein, Hugh saw the smoke billowed from the goat shed, now engulfed in flames. Fire was almost as feared as an enemy camped without the gates. Although the stone keep was not at risk, the flames could consume the stables, the kennels, the falconry, the barracks, the granary.

Flinging himself out of the saddle, Hugh roared a command at the line of men strung from the well to the shed. "Fill more buckets!"

With the added muscle of Hugh and his men-at-arms, the flames were soon doused. The charred remains of the goat shed still sizzled and spit when at last the lord of Exmoor demanded to know to what caused the blaze.

"It was me." His brother stepped forward, his boy's face streaked with soot and grime. "I set the fire."

"How?"

The question came like the lash of a whip. Guy flinched but didn't shirk from his brother's wrath.

"Jasmine was just… I mean, we were…" He stopped, drew in a breath, and squared his shoulders. "I asked her to show me how to throw her jeweled dagger."

Hugh's fulminating glance sliced to the girl as coated with soot as her accomplice. She was standing next to her sister and the other ladies who'd rushed to the scene.

"I didn't mean to overshoot the mark and send the curved handle into the shank of John Pigman's prize sow," Guy continued. "I swear I didn't."

The passionate declaration yanked Hugh's attention back to the lad.

"But my aim was off and the sow ran squealing at the exact moment the farrier led one of the warhorses out of the smithy."

"Then the horse rears." Jasmine picked the story a clear, ringing voice. Chin up, she stepped away from her sister's sheltering arm. "And the stupid animal, he kicks the coals from the washerwoman's fire into the goat shed."

Christ and all the saints! As if Hugh didn't have worries enough without having to deal with the near disastrous consequences of two irresponsible children. Before he could mete out punishment, however, Eleanor stepped into the breach.

"I don't know who led who into mischief, my lord, but you must see they intended no harm."

Still unsettled from the contentious enclave at Chester, Hugh was in no mood to be instructed in what he must and must not do in his own keep. His jaw tight, he faced the woman. "You would tell me how to assess this situation?"

"No! I would not so presume."

"That's wise of you."

He thought the matter settled and was searching his mind for the proper punishment when she stepped into the fray once again.

"But they are children, my lord. Surely you…"

"Enough."

She blinked at the curt command but stood her ground. "I can see from your fearsome scowl it's not enough."

Her refusal to yield the field astounded him and everyone else present. A low murmur raced through the crowd, near lost against the snap and crackle of the dying fire.

Hugh issued a last, low warning. "I will hear no more from you, lady"

Eleanor cast a swift glance at her sister. Although Jasmine had her chin angled and a mulish look on her face, the child was frightened. Years of standing as both mother and sister to the headstrong girl stiffened Eleanor's spine. She could see Hugh was not moved to let either Jasmine or Guy off lightly for their misdeeds. It was up to her, therefore, to plead their cause.

"But hear me you must."

She employed the same firm but cajoling tone she'd so often used on her errant father. She saw at once, however, it didn't works as well in this instance. The shocked gasps that rose from the crowd in the bailey gave her pause. So did the ice that coated Exmoor's blue eyes. Despite herself, she took a step back as he moved forward and skewered her with a look that sucked the marrow from her bones.

"I will hear no more from you," he repeated softly, dangerously. "You will take yourself and your sister to the ladies' solar and remain there until I bid you leave."

He was so fearsome, so menacing, that Eleanor couldn't have forced another reply had she wanted to. Nor did Lady Alice give her the chance. With a hard yank on Eleanor's elbow, she dragged her away.

Lady Alice delivered the verdict not long afterward. The Lady Eleanor was to remain in the ladies' solar for a complete sweep of the sundial. Jasmine was to report to Father Anselem immediately to confess her sins and do penance for them.

"And Guy?" Eleanor asked, worried for the boy. "What punishment will he receive?"

"Hugh will decide that," Lady Alice said repressively.

Jasmine took the pronouncement with a sullen pout. Eleanor on the other hand was profoundly grateful that their punishment wasn't worse. When Eleanor tried to thank Lady Alice, however, the older woman offered a piece of tart advice.

"My son will be pushed only so far. I would counsel you both to remember that in the future."

She departed the solar leaving both sisters to reflect on their much changed circumstances. Eleanor swallowed her chagrin and managed to present a calm demeanor. Jasmine was far less reconciled to her situation.

"These English," she said angrily when she returned to the solar some hours later, after confessing her transgression and doing penance for it. "They're swine."

"They're Norman," Eleanor corrected in an effort to distract her. "As much French as they are English."

"Pah! They're swine, whatever their roots." She whirled, a diminutive dervish with her skirts swirling and her eyes fierce. "No desert lord be so cruel as to confine you to your chamber, Sister."

Wisely, Eleanor chose not to remind her that most desert lords confined their women to harems, where they were immured for a lifetime instead of mere hours. It was best not to stoke her sister's temper when it flamed.

"Catherine thinks the same," Jasmine declared.

"Catherine?"

"She was there in the chapel when I did my penance, fingering her rosary and murmuring the most heart-rending prayers to the Virgin. When I asked her why, she got all weepy and muttered something about a woman's duty."

Eleanor's heart twisted. Catherine's terror of marriage and the wifely duties it entailed struck deep indeed. Sighing for the girl and her inevitable fate, she patted the cushioned window seat.

"Come, sit with me," she said to her sister, "and I'll tell you tales of grand viziers and handsome princes turned into sand lizards by evil *jinni*."

The fantastical tales soothed Jasmine's ruffled feathers and would have kept her in the ladies' solar had not her healthy young appetite recalled her to her grievances.

"Does Exmoor mean to starve us?" she asked after her stomach gave a ferocious rumble.

Eleanor dared not give the child added cause to rebel against the man who now held sway over them both. "Of course not," she said with forced cheer. "You may go down to supper as you will. Lady Alice said she would send me a tray."

Her sister's lower lip jutted out. "It's not right, Ella. You had naught to do with the fire."

"True, but I was so bold as to challenge a lord in his own keep. My temper ran away with me. As yours must not," she added sternly when the girl shoved away from he window seat. "Mind your tongue, eat your dinner, and return to the solar at once. Do you hear me? Jasmine! Do you hear me?"

"Aye."

Eleanor watched her sister leave with a dire sense of foreboding. The feeling only increased as the next hour passed with agonizing slowness. Not even the heavily laden tray and flagon of wine delivered to the bower soothed her nerves. She'd just signaled to a page to remove the tray when her worst fears were realized.

"Eleanor!"

An irate Lady Alice burst in, towing Jasmine with her. Lady Catherine and a bevy of other women crowded in behind them.

"You must do something with this child," Lady Alice fumed.

"Oh, lud. What now?"

"What now? What *now*?"

Recognizing that her voice had reached a near screech, the older woman released Jasmine and strove for calm. "She waylaid the page serving the high table and dropped a toad in my son's goblet."

Groaning, Eleanor addressed her unrepentant sister. "You did not!"

"I did," the girl confirmed defiantly. "And I whispered incantations over it first. They may not work in this thrice-damed clime. But if they do, Exmoor will be all over warts on the morrow."

Eleanor couldn't help but be proud of her fearless young sister even as her mind worked feverishly on how to avert another, harsher punishment.

"What did Hugh do when he discovered the toad?" she asked his indignant mother.

"He fished it out and put it in his pocket," Lady Alice retorted. "None of us at the high table would've been any the wiser if it hadn't jumped out and onto the table, causing Catherine to squeal in fright."

Exmoor's young bride flushed and tears flooded her brown eyes. "It was such an ugly little toad. I...I could not help myself."

Eleanor made haste to assure her that most damsels would squeal if a toad jumped onto the table. In truth, though, she was more concerned about how to spare Jasmine more hours on her knees than assuaging Catherine's watery tears.

"Lady Alice, I beg you to take a message to your son. Give me but a moment to pen it."

Eleanor cast a quick look around the bower but the only writing implement she spotted was the fine-tipped charcoal pencil Sir Gile's wife used to trace patterns on fabrics. She snatched up the pencil and a scrap of cloth, thought a moment, and composed a brief note.

"Please, give this to your son."

"Very well." The older woman's lips firmed as she cast a fulminating glance at the still unrepentant miscreant. "Until you have his answer, I suggest you and your sister remain abovestairs. Come, Catherine, we'd best return to the table."

A page delivered a response to Eleanor's missive within the hour. To her relief, Exmoor agreed to her request for a private audience. She could ride out with him on the morrow when he went to check the sheep shearing, the curt note related. *After* her period of confinement had ended.

The high-handed reply rankled, but Eleanor tried to calm both herself and Jasmine. She truly tried. To one used to coming and going as she pleased, however, the rest of the evening passed with the speed of a plodding ox.

The next day was worse. Morning dragged toward noon. Noon crawled by. Finally Hugh sent a request that Lady Eleanor join him at the stables.

She'd dressed in one of her older gowns in anticipation of his summons. The leaf green bliaut had unfashionably loose sleeves that reached only to her knees and a square neckline cut low to show her linen under-dress. Her blue ankle boots were new, though, and she'd covered her braided hair with a veil anchored by a circlet of corded silk. Thus armored, Eleanor felt prepared for the battle ahead.

Exmoor waited for her in the bailey. Instead of chain mail and a surcoat emblazoned with his eagle, he wore plain leather breeks and a tanned leather jerkin over a linen shirt. His sword rode low on his hip, but he'd left off his helm so that his hair gleamed like polished oak in the July sun. He'd taken the precaution of mounting a small troop to accompany them, though.

Eleanor gave Sirocco only a short, longing glance before addressing the lord who stood ready to mount her on what looked like a docile and well-mannered palfrey.

"I thank you for agreeing to speak with me privately," she said.

"You may wish to reserve your gratitude until after I hear what you have to say."

"As you will."

The demure reply sent his brows soaring. "Had I known a day and night of reflection would render you so amenable, lady, I might have ordered it sooner rather than later."

He was teasing her. She knew that. Still, she had to bite her tongue to keep from informing him just how un-amenable that day and night had rendered her.

He didn't fail to note her heroic effort, and his mouth curved in a way that made Eleanor bite down harder on her abused tongue. Still grinning, he signaled to the groom to position her palfrey at the mounting block.

"Shall we ride, lady?"

Chapter Six

Eleanor was so happy to be outside the keep's walls that she swallowed her chagrin at the palfrey's docile manner and plodding gait. Willing herself not to cast covetous glances at Sirocco's sleek lines and smooth moves, she studied the countryside they traveled through with appreciative eyes. To one reared in the harsh desert, the thick forests and ripe green fields presented a lush landscape.

She said little, however, until they approached a cluster of mud-and-wattle huts. Hugh stopped some yards from a penned enclosure where a crowd of peasants was engaged in the sweaty business of shearing sheep. The smell was thick and musty, and the clamor worse than the shouts and wails of merchants in an Eastern bazaar. Ewes baaed as the women dragged them from the pen. Lambs bleated piteously for their dams. Men shouted and cursed as they flipped sheep this way and that, and shears flashed as the animals were rid of their wool with a speed that made Eleanor marvel.

When the shearers spotted Hugh, they paused in their labors and tugged off their caps. He acknowledged them with a smile and waved them back to work. As the dust and noise erupted again, an overseer with the distinctive Exmoor eagle on his vest detached himself from the busy group. He conferred with Hugh for a few moments before noticing Eleanor's wide-eyed fascination. Smiling, he offered a brief tutorial.

"The flocks were culled in May, lady, and the lambs weaned. We sheared the sheep selected for market then, and put them out to pasture to fatten them. This lot provided milk for sweet cheese these past weeks. But now we've dunked them in yon stream to remove the accumulated filth from their fleeces so we can take their wool."

"What will you do with all that?" she asked, as fascinated by mountain of fluffy gray.

"The shearers may do as they wish with their portion. Spin it or sell it, as their needs dictate. The rest we take to market." A note of gruff pride crept into his voice as he turned to his master. "The demesne portion will be twice what it was last year, lord. We've lost far fewer ewes since you allowed the peasants to hunt the bear and catamounts that feed on them."

Eleanor glanced at her companion in surprise. In Outremer, hunting lion and panther and other large game was a privilege reserved exclusively for lords and knights. Even the taking of feathered prey with falcons and hawks was restricted to the nobility. Her father had led her to believe the same customs held in the West. According to him, any who dared to poach in a lord's domains risked penalties ranging from the loss of an eye or a hand to hanging from the nearest tree.

"Will you join us for the shearing supper?" his bailiff wanted to know.

"I cannot. But given your assurance of a bountiful clipping, I'll tell the ale master to send extra barrels for the feast."

The promise earned a happy grin from the bailiff and a cheer from the others when it was relayed. Still marveling at the shearers' speed, Eleanor waved farewell.

The noise and dust faded into the background as the small troop followed a track through a dense copse. When the escort trailed behind, she took advantage of the relative privacy to broach the topic that weighed heavy in her breast.

"About the toad…"

"Aye?"

"Jasmine thought only to avenge what she considered an unjust punishment for my speaking out on her behalf."

"And you, lady? Do you consider it unjust?"

With some effort, Eleanor fought to moderate her response. "I understand that I should not have challenged you in front of others."

"You understand? But you don't agree?"

"No, I do not. But I'm sorry my forwardness, lord."

She expected him to accept the apology with some measure of graciousness. She *wasn't* expecting his snort. When she flashed him an indignant glance, his blue eyes glinted.

"I'm amazed those words didn't choke you."

She stiffened, unwilling to admit how close he'd come to the truth. Then her sense of the ridiculous rescued her. Laughing, she conceded the point. "They did, in truth, come near to strangling me. But, please, hear me out. If you think to visit more punishment on Jasmine than a few hours with Father Anselem, I would ask that you visit on me instead."

"Why you?" He tilted his head. "How is it that you bear such responsibility for her?"

Eleanor let the palfrey plod alongside Sirocco while she stitched her thoughts together. "Our father, Jasmine's and mine, was…"

She searched for the words to describe their sire.

"He was easy of heart," she finished with considerable understatement. "Not on the battlefield or in tourney," she hurried to add. "In his youth, Queen Eleanor herself awarded him a silken purse for besting one of her knights. I'm named for her, you know."

"I assumed as much. And…" Exmoor prompted when she fell silent, lost in her memories.

"And," she continued with a wry smile, "my sire was somewhat fond of both wine and games of chance. I cannot tell you how many times I had to visit a money lender to cover his gaming losses or redeem his sword and armor."

"You dealt with moneylenders yourself?"

She had to laugh at the surprise and disapproval in his voice. "Oh, aye. Often. There was one - a kindly, bewhiskered Jew - who refused to charge me interest on the sums I came to pay him."

This same gentle soul had been brutally murdered during one of the not-infrequent waves of violence against non-believers in the Christian kingdom of Jerusalem. Stifling a sigh at the memory, Eleanor returned to her main concern.

"My father won Jasmine's mother on a throw of the dice. She was desert bred and quite fierce. I went to bed each night expecting to wake the next morning and find my father with his throat cut. By some miracle, he survived. And she disappeared the same day she dropped his babe."

Finding that tiny, squalling bundle was a memory that would stay with Eleanor always. She'd been just a girl herself, not yet ten years old, but she became a mother as well as a sister that day.

"So you see, Jasmine is more than just my father's get on a slave girl. She's the child of my heart."

"And your father? Was she the child of his heart, too?"

Eleanor's peal of laughter startled a pair of wood doves from their perch. Wings flapping, they darted into the hot air.

"Our father was wont to say Jasmine was put on earth for the sole purpose of bedeviling his last years. When he wasn't hiring out his sword to some lord or emir, he would usually retreat to the wineshops to escape us."

"Escape?" Exmoor echoed drily.

"I took charge of our household even before I learned to count." She heaved an exaggerated sigh. "I fear I have a somewhat over managing disposition."

"Somewhat?"

"How unkind of you to chuff me, sir, when I'm trying to be so penitent."

Hugh threw her another look. If that was penitence in those forest green eyes, he would stew his leather gauntlets and have them for supper.

"About the toad," she said, returning to the topic that had prompted her request for private discourse. "Lady Alice said it frightened Catherine. For that both Jasmine and I are truly sorry."

He allowed no hint of the frustration he so often experienced when dealing with his betrothed to show in his face or his voice. "Catherine is a young and gentle maid. But she worked up the courage to come to me this morning and beg me not to punish Jasmine for the prank."

"How brave of her! Mayhap she's not as timid as I've thought her."

When Hugh cocked a brow, heat rushed into Eleanor's cheeks.

"Curse my tongue! Your promised wife has been most kind and generous. I didn't mean to disparage her. I ask your pardon."

"Granted."

"So…? So you will not mete out additional punishment on Jasmine for the toad?"

"I will not. I've no desire to crush her spirit, any more than I do Guy's. But be warned…I won't be as forbearing in the future. You'd best keep her on a tighter rein."

"I shall certainly endeavor to do so," she said in a voice that didn't give either of them much hope for future success.

That uncomfortable matter dealt with, Eleanor relaxed and let herself enjoy the ride. They followed the path through the dappled woods in silence for a while, until a new sound gradually emerged above the twitter of birds and the thump of iron-shod hooves on the dirt track. Hardly more than a muted whisper at first. Then a soft gurgle. Finally the path curved and the woods opened to reveal a precipitous drop to a wide river. It flowed below them, the bright sunlight glinting off its surface as it splashed around granite boulders and outcroppings of fallen trees.

Eleanor had only to look on the cool, rippling water to feel the heat of the July sun burning her face. "What river is this?"

"The Alyn. A tributary of the mighty Dee."

"And that?" she asked, pointing to a humped shape beached high on the rock-strewn river bank.

Hugh leaned forward and followed the line of her arm until he spotted what looked like an overturned walnut shell.

"That, lady, is what the Welsh call a *cwrwgl*. A boat made of interwoven willow rods covered with hide." He rested his hands on the pommel. "Fishermen have used the coracle to navigate these swift flowing rivers for centuries. Julius Caesar described them in his account of his invasion of Britain."

"Truly?"

"Truly." A sardonic smile tipped his lips. "To his and all subsequent invaders' dismay, only a true Welshman can maneuver the damned things. Many a Norman has taken a dunking trying."

"Are you one of those Normans?"

"I was," he admitted ruefully, "until one of the local fishermen taught me to steer it."

The river called to her. Unlike the broad, mud-brown wadis of the land she'd called home until a few months ago, these waters beckoned green and cool and irresistible.

"Show me," she challenged with a teasing glint in her eyes.

Every instinct Hugh possessed warned him to ignore the gauntlet she'd just thrown down. He hadn't paddled a coracle in years. Even then he'd been a clumsy oarsman at best. Yet his shirt was sticking to his back beneath his leather jerkin and he knew from many a boyhood swim how good the river would feel against his sweaty skin.

Twisting in the saddle, he signaled to the sergeant of his small troop. "The Lady Eleanor and I are going to take to the water in that coracle."

The sergeant's brows hooked but he was too well trained to do more than nod an acknowledgment.

"Send two men to patrol down river," Hugh instructed. "Then bring our horses to the bend where the tumbled rocks form a backwater. You know the place?"

"Aye, lord."

"Wait for us there."

He helped Eleanor dismount and escorted her down a barely discernible path to the river's rock-strewn bank. When he flipped the coracle over, his doubts about his ability to maneuver the flat-bottomed, hide-covered basket came rushing back. It was too late to back out now, though. He'd already accepted the challenge.

The stink of the tarred hide wrinkled Eleanor's nose. Hugh fully expected her to back away at that point. But when he shoved the craft to the river's edge and sent her a questioning look, she hiked up her skirts, waded into the shallows, and stepped into the shell.

"Sit there," he instructed with a jerk of his chin, "with your back against the rim."

She sank down cautiously and stretched her arms along the rough bark rim. When she had a good grip, Hugh pushed the coracle deeper. Clear, cool water sloshed over his boots and swirled up to his knees. He pushed further, feeling slightly ridiculous. As if he were Guy, escaping from Father Anselem for a few hours of play.

Then the current caught the coracle, and his ever-present responsibilities as Lord of Exmoor receded. For these stolen moments, at least, he would enjoy the sun and the river and the companionship of this alluring woman.

With a lithe move, he swung aboard. The basket rocked violently, causing Eleanor to gasp and clutch the rim more tightly. Thankfully, the coracle steadied as Hugh dropped cross-legged to the flat bottom and found a comfortable position between the thick willow ribs. The paddle was wedged under another rib. While he wrestled it free, the boat bounced and whirled on the current.

Eleanor gripped the edge with white-knuckled fists but only laughed when he thrust the paddle into the water and doused her with an inadvertent splash.

"Your pardon!"

"I don't mind it. The wet feels good."

Using the paddle as a rudder he aimed the little boat deeper into the current. It still swirled and bounced, but not as violently as before.

"How can anyone catch a fish with the boat bobbing so?" Eleanor wanted to know.

"The fishermen usually work in pairs, each in his own coracle. They'll paddle one handed, and with the other they hold the end of a net. As the current carries them downstream, the net scoops in their catch."

She peered cautiously over the side. "What kind of catch?"

"Brown trout, mostly, and salmon in season. Just a year ago, two men from the village pulled a thirty pound salmon out of the river."

"Thirty pounds! It must have put up quite a fight. However did they get such a monster aboard?"

"When they have a large catch like that, each man will haul on their end of the net until their boats touch and the fish is trapped. Then one will stun it with a wooden mallet and haul it in."

As he picked up the river's rhythm, the half-forgotten tricks he'd learned so long ago returned. He leaned back against the rim and adjusted the paddle's angle to guide the little craft around rocks and fallen trees with their branches stripped bare and trunks bleached white. Eleanor gradually relaxed her death grip and twisted to scan the rippling waters ahead. At the sound of a distant, muted roar, she sent Hugh a quick look.

"What do I hear?"

"Rapids."

"Do we ride them?"

"We should not. I must've been about Guy's age the last time I last dared them."

"Ah, yes. And you're so bent and wheezing now. Much wiser to give them pass."

By *Jesu!* Eve must have had just that teasing note in her voice when she tempted Adam.

"Vixen."

Her face was all innocence. "Do you speak of me, lord?"

"Aye, lady, I do."

She appeared to consider that for a moment before a grin slipped out. "Does that mean we ride the rapids?"

"It does. But I'll hear no recriminations if you take a dunking."

"You have my word on it."

"Hold tight, then."

The ride was wild and wet and so exhilarating that not a single word of blame escaped Eleanor's lips when a submerged rock tipped both her and Hugh into the river. It wasn't deep, barely up to her waist, but the current was strong enough to take her under. She floundered for a few moments before she came up gasping. Fighting the river's pull, she helped Hugh drag the overturned coracle out of the water, then dropped onto the mossy bank.

She'd lost her circlet and veil. Straggling strands of wet hair escaped her braid and were draped across her face and shoulders. She suspected the new leather half boots that had given her such delight were ruined, and her soaked bliaut clung to her like a second skin.

Yet for the first time since arriving at Exmoor Keep, she felt lighthearted and free of the worries that had forced her to leave the land of her birth. Free, too, of the burden of securing a future for herself and Jasmine. And free, *so* free, of the rigid restrictions that governed the life of the women residing at the keep.

She stretched out on the sun-warmed lichen and bent one elbows behind her head. Her other hand toyed with the silver key that had slipped from its nest between her breasts The sky above her was a bright, searing blue, while the trees crowding the river showed a dozen different shades of green. She could grow to love this land, she thought. It was as unlike the Levant as a war horse was to an ass. Yet it pulled at something deep inside her.

She knew little of her mother aside from the fact she'd been a lady in service to Queen Melisende. But her father had been born here, in England. Mayhap Eleanor had inherited more than his green eyes and ready laugh. Mayhap this verdant, fertile land was in her blood.

She would find a husband of the same blood, she vowed. And not just to settle herself and Jasmine. Much as it shamed her to admit it, the sinful cravings that had on occasion disturbed her sleep were growing more frequent. She longed to join her body as well as her future to a husband's. One strong and virile enough to satisfy these vague, distracting needs. Needs that seemed to have grown even more urgent since she'd come to Exmoor.

They crept up on her now, as if summoned by the devil himself. A spear of heat. A tight, swift curl low in her belly. She refused to angle her head. Would not allow her glance to seek the man stretched out beside her. But she knew well he was the cause of much of the restless that invaded her sleep of late.

To her dismay, the stubborn will so often lamented by her father now failed her. She angled her head. Slid her gaze sideways. And felt her heart jolt inside her chest.

Exmoor leaned on one elbow. His hair was damp, gleaming like polished oak in the sun. His eyes feasted on her face. They were so blue, so intense behind wet, spiked lashes. For the space of a heartbeat, mayhap two, Eleanor saw the same hunger now gnawing at her insides reflected in his dark pupils.

It was gone almost before she recognized it for what it was. In the next breath he'd wiped all expression from his face. Then he coiled his legs under him and pushed to his feet. When he turned and reached down a hand to help her up, she saw nothing but polite courtesy in the gesture.

"My troop will begin to wonder what befell us, lady. We'd best join them."

She took his hand and rose. When he loosed his grip, she shook out the folds of her soggy skirts and eyed the upturned boat. "Do we take to the river again?"

"I think not. The backwater where the men await us is just around the bend. We'll leave the coracle here and walk."

The companionship and laughter of those shared moments on the river were gone. Eleanor felt their loss like a stone on her heart but understood the necessity for his deliberate withdrawal.

She'd seen his desire, if only for that brief instant. As he'd no doubt seen hers. She knew as well as he that naught could come that forbidden hunger. Naught *would* come of it.

With a nod, she matched her tone to his. "As you will."

Five minutes walk along the riverbank brought them to the spot where the troop waited. As Hugh had expected, his men gaped at their wet lord and the bedraggled lady accompanying him. He took a good-natured gibe from his sergeant-at-arms about the overturned coracle and arranged to have word of its present location sent to it owner.

Then he lifted Eleanor into the saddle. Calmly. Deliberately. He didn't allow his hands to linger on her waist. Didn't let his gaze dwell on the length of calf and thigh molded by her wet skirts. But damned if it didn't take most of the ride back to the keep to empty his head of the image of her lying in careless abandon on the lichen, her arms above her head, and her wet bodice following the ripe curves of her breasts.

By the time they rode through the gates, Hugh knew what he must do. He took the first step on that path by making a polite request when he lifted Eleanor from the saddle.

"I would speak with you when you have recovered from our swim," he told her. "Will you meet me in the counting room after Vespers?"

A question leapt into her eyes but she merely nodded. "Of course."

When Eleanor entered the ladies' solar, her wild hair and still damp gown produced surprise and exclamations. Lady Alice led the chorus.

"Sweet Virgin! What happened?"

"Hugh and I took a boat out on the river. A coracle, he called it."

"A coracle?" his mother echoed blankly. "Why ever would you get into one of those foul-smelling little baskets?"

How could she explain that the sun had decorated the water with a thousand sparkling lights? That the current ran cool and fast? That those moments of bobbing and bouncing with Hugh had given her more pleasure than anything else she'd experienced since her arrival?

"Your son wished to show me how these Welsh craft were rowed."

"But your gown! You new boots!"

"I know," she replied, laughing. "As it happens, coracles are not as easily maneuvered as your son recalled. We tipped over mid-stream."

"Holy Virgin!" Catherine went as pale as the altar cloth she'd been embroidering and hurriedly made the sign of the Cross. "You might have drowned."

"Hardly. The water came only to my waist. Now I must change. And if you would be so kind, Lady Alice, would you send a page to find Jasmine. I must speak with her."

Her sister rushed into the bower as Eleanor was lacing the sides of a clean, dry bliaut. Rather than voice any of the concern displayed by Lady Alice and Catherine, she was extremely unhappy about the fact that Eleanor had enjoyed such a splendid adventure when she'd been stuck in the dim, stuffy chancel.

"Why must I memorize Psalms when you get to swim in the river?" she complained, arms crossed and foot tapping. "Father Anselem is kind, yes, and patient, but his Latin is not as true as that we speak at home. I must correct him often."

Eleanor swallowed a groan. She'd best take the priest a special gift. An offering from her little chest to soothe his feeling at being tutored by a child. She still had the handkerchief-wrapped ruby that Exmoor had refused to take tucked away.

"Be thankful all you have to do is memorize Psalms. I spoke with Sir Hugh today while we were…"

"Swimming in the river!"

"…while we were out. He assured me he won't impose any further punishment for your silly prank with that toad. But you must behave, Jasmine. He won't turn a blind eye to disruptions of his household or scurry off to a wine shop when your temper flares, as our father did."

"I only sought to avenge the insult to you!"

"I know, sweeting, I know. But I can fight my own battles. Promise me you'll at least stop and think before you do anything so outrageous again."

"I'll stop," she said mutinously. "I'll think. But…"

"Serve me no 'buts'!"

Jasmine blinked in surprise. She was unused to hearing such a sharp tone from her sister. Then the forest green eyes she'd inherited from their father filled with tears.

Smothering the motherly instincts that rushed to the fore, Eleanor modified her tone but didn't sweep the girl into a forgiving hug as she might otherwise have done.

"Do you promise?"

Her sister's lips stayed mutinously tucked between her teeth.

"Jasmine! Do you promise?"

"Aye."

With the summer sun riding so high, it was still light outside when supper was served. After which, Eleanor and Jasmine joined the rest of the residents of the hall for Vespers. The time-honored verses were chanted, hymns were sung, psalms were recited, and Father Anselem read a passage. Eleanor joined in the signing of the Magnificat - the canticle to the Blessed Virgin - and said a fervent *pater noster*.

As Jasmine had asserted, the Latin sounded quite different from that of the Holy Land, where priests from so many different countries adopted the rhythm and cadence of those who lived and prayed where Christ had once walked. Eleanor ignored Jasmine's I-told-you-so glance when Father Anselem twisted several Latin verbs and waited only until she'd sent the girl up to the women's bower before asking a page to escort her once again to the counting room.

As on her first visit, the cellar offered up a host of different scents. The smell of tanned leather and oiled chain mail in the armory. The stink of despair and excrement from the dungeons. The waft of pepper and cardamon and cinnamon from the padlocked storeroom.

And as before, Exmoor was waiting for her in the counting room. He stood at the scarred oak table used for sorting coins and keeping records. Eleanor spotted her own small cask amid the chests stacked behind him and reminded herself to make an offering to Father Anselem when Exmoor had finished his business with her.

At her entrance, Hugh looked up from the parchment he'd been studying. Like her, he'd changed after his unplanned swim. The short, sleeveless tunic was trimmed with an exquisite band of embroidery that was plainly Lady Alice's handiwork. That was worn over a linen shirt and knitted hose that clung to his muscled calves.

He dismissed the page who'd escorted her and wasted little time explaining the reason for this meeting. "Since you've made it plain that you desire a husband, I've decided to endow you with land and silver enough to attract one suitable to your station."

Chapter Seven

"Endow me?" Eleanor repeated.

"Aye."

Hugh could read the emotions chasing across her face as clearly as the phases of the moon. First, surprise. Then confusion. Then a flush of anger.

He could guess what fed that flush. She must know why he proposed to dower her. She was no timid wood-mouse like his betrothed. She'd seen the lust that gripped him this afternoon. Sense the hunger that even now twisted his belly. She must understand as well as he that it was best for her to marry and remove herself from Exmoor before lust spilled into sin.

But Christ's bones! If she was not under his protection...

If he was not promised to Catherine...

"Why would you dower me?"

"Our kinship is distant, but I would see you well provided for."

"We share no kinship."

"You're the daughter of my mother's cousin-by-marriage and living in my household. Thus you're my responsibility until you pass to someone I deem able to provide you the same measure of protection."

"Someone *you* deem able?"

"Who else but me? You're newly arrived in England. You don't know the worth or reputation of any man who might court you. And you yourself said that you wanted my guidance in this matter."

"Guidance, yes! But..."

She muttered a few words that Hugh guessed were Arabic. He also guessed they were less than complimentary.

"I should have remained in the East. There, at least, I could've had my pick of second sons and landless mercenaries. Now, apparently, you think to direct my choice."

"Come, Eleanor, let's not brangle over the color of the horse before it's brought to market." Impatient now, he gestured to the parchment. "I wished only to tell you that I've drawn up a charter granting you a small property some leagues from here and a bride chest of sixty silver marks."

Her chin lifted. "I thank you, but I require neither your lands nor your silver."

"You do," he shot back, "if all you have to bring a husband are a sharp tongue and that ruby you showed me."

"Indeed?"

He reined in his irritation with her lack of gratitude and tempered his tone. "Forgive me. That was unkind. Of course, you would bring a husband much more. You have a merry laugh, and your wit is as sharp as your tongue. And God knows you are woman enough to stir any man's desire."

He meant only to offer a compliment. Yet as soon as the words were out, they conveyed a far different message than he'd intended. Her eyes darkened, and he knew she was thinking of the dangerous heat that had kindled between them this afternoon. For a long moment their glances held, and neither moved for fear of adding fuel to that smoldering spark.

Then she gave her head a little shake. "May I have my casket?"

"What?"

She gestured to the small chest stacked atop the others behind him. "The casket I left with you for safekeeping. May I have it, please?"

Yielding to the abrupt command, Hugh retrieved the chest and placed it on the table. A frown creased his brow as she tugged on the thin silver chain she wore around her neck. When it slipped free of its nest between her breasts, a small key dangled at its end. She twisted the key in the casket's lock, threw back the lid, and extracted a silken purse. A swift yank loosened the strings. Another jerk dumped the contents on the table,

"*Jesu*!"

Stunned, Hugh stared at the pile of loose, glittering rubies. While he viewed them in disbelief, Eleanor scooped more treasures from the casket. A ring with an emerald as large as her thumb. A wide collar studded with the same green stones. A girdle of woven gold links, adorned with sapphires and pearls. There were bangles, too, of gold and silver and precious jade.

"These are all from that sultan you spoke of?" he asked incredulously.

"The sultan of J'bara, yes."

"Because your father took the arrow meant for him?"

"The rubies were indeed a blood gift. These other jewels were gifts to entice me to join his harem."

Once again, erotic images leaped unbidden into Hugh's head. Kohl-rimmed emerald eyes smiling seductively above a silken veil. A half-vest that revealed more than it covered of high, firm breasts. Slender legs gleaming pearl white through the transparent trews such odalisques were rumored to wear. It took near all he had to banish the images and attend to what Eleanor was saying.

"The emeralds will be Jasmine's dowery. The sapphires and pearls I hope to pass to my daughters, should I have any." She stirred the rubies with the tip of a finger. "And these should buy me a suitable husband, should they not?"

"Of a certainty they will, but not, mayhap, one you would choose."

"How so?"

"You've heard the talk. Although not yet crowned king, Richard is bleeding his barons dry to fund his Crusade."

"Ah, yes, the Saladin tax everyone complains about."

"But he needs more. Far more. And, as you yourself just pointed out, your tie to Exmoor is not one of blood." He waved a hand over the scattered jewels. "If word of this rich cache gets out, the king could decide to make you and Jasmine wards of the crown and take charge of your estate until he sells you both to the highest bidder. Or..."

He hesitated, loathe to burden her with the harsh realities. But she guessed the third, very possible, course of action.

"Or the king could well decide to send us to a nunnery and add these pretty baubles to his own treasury."

"He could," Hugh agreed grimly. "So we must get you wedded and bedded before he learns of these riches."

The blunt response leached some of the color from her cheeks. But she tipped her chin and returned a cool reply. "I agree. But how do I accomplish it in such haste?"

"*You* will do nothing. I, however, will let it be known that I've dowered a young and comely kinswoman." He whipped up a palm to forestall her protest. "No, don't flail up at me! I'll add the demesne we discussed to your jewels. But we won't let the precise details of your estate circulate until a worthy suitor has presented himself."

"How will I attract someone worthy if all I have to offer is a small holding?"

"Don't forget your merry laugh."

"Aye, and my sharp tongue!"

"Yes, but that's something you must try to hide from your quarry until he's well and truly snared." He had to smile at her sputter of indignation. "I jest, Eleanor. I jest. The fact that you're under my protection will deter any suitors I consider unworthy."

She cocked her head. "And if our opinions on a suitor's worthiness differ?"

Confound the woman. She would argue with Saint Peter at the gates of Heaven!

"You don't trust my judgement?"

"In most matters," she conceded reluctantly. "As long as you agree that I have the final word in who I take as husband."

As if he would force her - or any woman - into a man's bed. Still, the comment bit too close to the bone. Reminded of Catherine's deep-seated fear, he nodded curtly. "Agreed."

"Good," she said briskly. "Now I ask again, how do we go about this?"

He gave up trying to convince her to leave the matter in his hands. She would command her own destiny, will he or nil he.

"I'll host a tourney in honor of Catherine's name day. It comes in the second week of August."

At which point, Hugh thought grimly, she would be well past the age the Church deemed permissible for bedding. He was fast running out of excuses for not consummating his thrice-damned betrothal. The realization twisted his gut even as he addressed his mind to the matter of Eleanor's marriage.

"I'll speak to my lady mother tonight and dispatch heralds tomorrow announcing the tourney. There won't be time to send word much farther than Chester and York, but rumors will most assuredly spread of the beauteous young kinswoman under my protection."

Her lids flickered at the compliment but she made no remark other than to thank him as she tipped the rubies back into their silken pouch. Once the casket was locked, she tucked the dangling key that dangled inside the neckline of her gown. Then Hugh returned the small box to its place atop his money chest and escorted her abovestairs.

The next morning he requested a private audience with his mother. She joined him in the lord's chamber, hot and flushed from overseeing the firing of the cauldrons in the yard for the monthly wash of bed linens.

"I swear by all the saints," she muttered as she tucked a sweaty tendril inside her drooping wimple, "the kitchen maids would sooner sleep with fleas than boil the pallet covers before we stuff them with fresh straw."

"You should let Sir Gile's wife oversee that task," Hugh scolded gently. "Or Catherine."

"Ha! The girl's as useful as.." She broke off and bit her lip. "I beg pardon, Hugh. Catherine tries to assume her duties as chatelaine. She *does* try. She's just so…so…"

"Timid?"

"Timid," Lady Alice agreed on a sigh. Sinking on to a bench, she regarded her son with a loving, if exasperated, eye. "Mayhap once you make your marriage to her real, she'd find the confidence to assume her role as wife."

Hugh rubbed two fingers along the bridge of his nose. He'd had this discussion with his mother before. Many times. She knew well the reason for Catherine's terror of the marriage bed but even her kindly heart was wearing thin of sympathy.

"I have no desire to breach her maidenhead by force," he stated, not for the first time.

"And how," his parent retorted, "do you intend to breed sons on the girl if you *don't* breach it?"

"I'll do what must be done," he conceded grimly, "when the time is right. But that's not why I asked to speak with you."

"Why then?"

"The Lady Eleanor wishes to be wed."

"Aye, I know. It's why she traveled all that way from the East. So we might help her find a suitable husband."

"And the sooner it's done, the better."

Something flickered in his mother's eyes. It was quickly come and just as quickly hidden when she glanced down and smoothed the folds of the rough-spun skirt she donned to oversee the cauldrons. When she lifted her gaze to his again, Hugh suspected she sensed there was more heat between him and Eleanor than either of them wished to acknowledge.

She merely nodded, however, and admitted that she'd given the matter of Eleanor's marriage some thought. "I have several knights in mind who might make a good match considering her lack of dowery."

"She'll be well dowered."

Her gaze narrowed. "So it's as urgent as that, is it?"

"Lady Mother…"

"Say no more!" She followed the abrupt command with a cool look. "I'm glad you mean to dower her. It's true Eleanor is no kin to you but she deserves better than her low estate would ordinarily command. What holding do you mean to confer on her?"

"Crynwyrth, with its mill and outlying farms."

She gave a brisk nod of approval. "Good! The rents alone will pay scutage for a knight and at least ten archers or spearmen. The mill another dozen. That should attract any number of suitors."

"That," he drawled, "and the jewels she brought back from the East with her."

"What jewels?"

"She gave me a casket for safekeeping when she first arrived," Hugh explained with a return of the disbelief that had gripped him the previous evening. "She showed me the contents last night. The chest holds a king's ransom in gems. Rubies. Emeralds. Sapphires and pearls so lustrous they gleam like the summer moon."

His mother gaped at him. "But…? How did she… Where did she…?"

Taking pity on her open-mouthed astonishment, he dropped down beside her on the bench and took both her hands in his. "As Eleanor herself said, it's a tale right out of *Arabian Nights*."

That earned an exasperated huff. "Sweet Mother of God! Even Father Anselem can't keep Guy from strutting about the keep in his ridiculous turban and spouting fantastical stories from that book."

"This one is every bit as fantastical. But true."

Swiftly, Hugh related the rubies paid to Simon de Brac's daughter when her sire took an arrow meant for a rich sultan. He related as well the potentate's desire to add Eleanor to his harem. His mother's eyes grew rounder with each detail. Once over her astonishment, it didn't take her long to grasp the the implications of such a sumptuous dower.

"Queen Eleanor!" she breathed. "She's as rapacious as her son when it comes to filling the crown's coffers. When word gets out of this rich hoard, the queen will take our Eleanor into her keeping. She'll end up like Princess Alys, neither wife nor wanted."

Hugh had little concern to spare for Alys of France, who'd been betrothed to Richard since the age of eight and was rumored to have become mistress to his father, Henry.

"For that reason," he told his mother carefully, "we must make sure word of the treasure doesn't leak out."

Her hands gripped his, so tight her knuckles showed white. "We tread dangerous ground here, my son. We can't cheat the king of a bride price."

"I don't intend to cheat him. But neither do we need to brag of Eleanor's riches until I enter negotiations for her hand."

"Then how are we to accomplish that?"

"I thought to hold a tourney in honor of Catherine's name day."

"A tourney? But King Henry banned them."

"William Marshal said Queen Eleanor lifted the ban in Richard's name. I know it doesn't give you much time to prepare, but a tournament will allow me to gather knights I know and trust. We can make Eleanor known to them during the festivities. And," he added dryly, "the gathering will allow her look over the combatants. As the lady informed me, she would have a say in who she takes to her bed this time."

"Hugh! Does she think the choice is hers?"

"She does, subject to my approval."

His mother's gaze dropped to her lap. Her veined hands smoothed the folds of her skirt. When she lifted her eyes to his, a smile lingered in their faded blue depth.

"I, too, begged for a say in who I was given to in marriage, but my father had neither the time or the temperament to indulge such foolish female whims. All that mattered was that I went to a man of honor with a strong sword arm and sufficient properties." A mischievous dimple appeared in one cheek. "Little did he know when he chose your father for that I'd already made him my choice. I was young and sly and still beauteous enough to have my way without either of them ever being the wiser."

Hugh matched her smile. "Let's hope Eleanor is as clever."

"I don't doubt she will be. She knows her mind, that one." With a final brisk sweep down her skirts, Lady Alice pushed off the stool. "If we're to host a tourney in little more than a fortnight, you'd best send out couriers right away."

"I will."

"We'll need tents for the lists," she said, her mind already forging ahead. "Additional candles. Fresh rushes for the great hall. Extra tuns of wine and ale. Oh, and red dye. If this tourney is to be in Catherine's honor, she'll need a new gown."

"I'll send a scribe to your bower. Order what you will."

"Send him to the storeroom instead." She bustled to the door, the laundry cauldrons forgotten. "I need to count the barrels of salted herring and peppered hams."

With Lady Alice so busily engaged, Hugh went to tell Catherine of the plans for her name day. He found her in the herb garden behind the keep, snipping rosemary and thyme with the scissors attached to her girdle by a length of braided gold thread. A linen headband held dark hair back from her forehead, and the face beneath it was smooth and serene and sweetly beautiful… until she heard his approach and looked up.

Hugh swallowed a curse as nervousness stiffened her porcelain features. He gave no hint of the irritation that roused in him, though, as he told her of the proposed fete.

"A… A tourney," she stammered. "In *my* honor?"

"Yes, little mouse, for you."

"But why do we…?"

Her hand clenched, crushing the green stems bunched in her fist. The rosemary's pungent, pine-like scent hung on the hot air as every vestige of color drained from her cheeks.

"I know it's past time we sealed our vows," she whispered in a voice so low and ragged that he had to bend close to hear her. "Hosting a tourney to…to mark the occasion does me great honor."

"The tourney is to celebrate your name day. And to make the Lady Eleanor known to knights in search of a wife."

"Oh."

Her face cleared as if the sun had burst from behind a cloud. Or a prisoner had burst free of his chains, Hugh thought sourly.

"What a clever idea. Eleanor's so merry and quick, all manner of suitors will besiege her. But you must choose someone who'll value her wit and charm."

"I'll do my best," he drawled.

"And mayhap…" She hesitated, then took her courage into both dainty hands. "Mayhap I might dower her, Hugh. I've scarce touched the silver in my bride chests. You've been so kind and generous that aside Michaelmas gifts and alms for the poor, I've spent near to nothing. I'd be most happy to settle a portion on Eleanor."

Sweet *Jesu*! Did everyone at Exmoor wish to see the wench well married? Had she worked her way into every heart the way she had his? Hugh refused to acknowledge the guilt that traitorous thought stirred and gave his promised wife a warm smile.

"Eleanor has no need of your silver, Cat. She'll be well dowered."

She looked doubtful but it wasn't in her nature to argue or question authority. Then she suddenly slapped a palm to her cheek. "Holy Mary! Lady Alice must be all a-dither! I'd best find her and see what she would have me do."

Whirling, she flew down the dirt path between the rows of herbs.

Eleanor was descending the winding tower stairs from the ladies' bower when a flushed and flustered Catherine rushed up.

"You'll never guess," the girl announced breathlessly. "We're to host a tourney!"

"Yes, Hugh told me. To celebrate your name day. You must be thrilled to be feted at such an event."

"I am. Truly, I am. It's just…" She stopped and took her lower lip between her teeth. Excitement and dread warred in her expressive little face.

Eleanor could guess what put that fearful look in her brown eyes. This name day would announce to all and sundry that Catherine was well past the proscribed age to consummate her. marriage.

With a little jolt, Eleanor realized that her patience with Hugh's faint-hearted bride had run almost as thin as Lady Alice's. Couldn't the girl see the worth of the man she was promised to? Did she take no assurance from the gentle way he handled her? Did she not know how lucky she would be to wed someone as sure and strong as Hugh?

And with another jolt, she recognized what lay at the root of her impatience. Jealousy, green and ugly and sinful. Shame washed through her as she tightened her fist around the small stone gripped in it. "Forgive me, Catherine, I must find Father Anselem. Then I doubt not Lady Alice will put us both to work preparing for the tourney."

She brushed by the younger woman and wound down the narrow stone stairs. Shame continued to dog her as she made her way to the chancery. Lusting for another woman's promised husband was as bad as fornicating with him. *Almost* as bad, she corrected with a tight little twist to her belly.

She found the castle priest in the room that served as both schoolroom and records repository for all matters relating to the spiritual needs of the keep.

"Ah, Lady Eleanor, welcome. Are you looking for Jasmine? She's gone to find Guy." His eyes twinkled amid their web of wrinkles. "I'm afraid instruction in the Holy Scripture couldn't compete with the excitement of a tourney."

So the news had already penetrated the dim quiet of the chapel.

"It's you I came to speak to, Father. Or rather…" She extended her hand, palm up, and uncurled her fingers. "I came to give you this."

Even in the dimness, the ruby gleamed.

"What's this?" the priest asked in astonishment.

"A gift from Jasmine and me for your many kindnesses. And your forbearance," she added with a smile.

"But…? Where…? How…?"

"How did I come by it?" Eleanor gave him a much shortened version of the tale. "It was a gift from the emir whose life my father saved. Jasmine and I wish to give it as tithe."

"This is far beyond tithe!" He tried to fold her fingers over the stone. "You must keep it."

"Truly, father, it is only one of the stones we brought from the East."

"There are more?" the priest gasped.

"There are. More than enough to dower both Jasmine and me, thanks be to the Lord. And since I hope to find a husband among the knights who'll come to compete in the tourney, we may soon leave Exmoor." She dropped the gem into his rough-skinned palm. "You could have it set into the crucifix above the altar. Or sell it and give alms to the poor."

Murmuring thanks for the generous gift, he made the sign of the Cross over her. She bowed her head to accept the blessing, then hesitated. The ugly sin she'd acknowledged to herself a bit ago gnawed at her. She knew she should ask forgiveness for the jealousy that had wormed its way into her heart.

Yet she couldn't bring herself to admit to this kindly old priest the restless cravings that tormented her since she'd come to Exmoor. Cravings that had become centered more and more around the lord of the keep. Instead, she vowed fiercely as she left the chapel, she would use the tourney to choose a husband of her own, then get herself and Jasmine gone.

Chapter Eight

Fast riders set out the next morning to find the queen on progress, carrying a petition to allow Hugh Montmercy, Baron Exmoor, to host the first tournament in England since the ban was lifted. Anxious to build acceptance for Richard in the kingdom he so rarely visited, the queen readily granted the license. With a stiff fee, of course, to be paid into the king's coffers. Royal approval secured, Hugh sent out proclamations announcing the tournament and inviting knights to compete.

As July gave way to August, preparations for the event threw every resident of keep and its outlying villages into a near frenzy. Cooks instructed a small army of kitchen boys to cut and stack great piles of wood for the ovens and fires. Maids scoured every pan and cauldron. Others climbed on stools and ladders to beat the tapestries in the great hall with flat sided paddles to release accumulated dust, then scrubbed them with brushes to bring out their rich colors. Freshly laundered pallets were stuffed with clean straw and sweet smelling herbs for the high-born guests, while additional pallets were rolled up and left in readiness for the servants and attendants who'd find space to sleep where they could.

Fletchers and armorers and farriers worked feverishly to outfit Exmoor's household knights for the tourney. Mail was burnished, blades sharpened, spare lances brought up from the armory.

Hugh organized several hunts. He and his men returned with carcasses of wild boar, several does and a great stag. He also rode out with his falconers, who released their belled birds to swoop down on pigeon and quail and hares and squirrels to add to the larder.

The outlying manses and villages contributed to the preparations as well. A bevy of women stitched bright new barding for the competitors' mounts, as well as flags and silken banners for the tents and wooden stalls their menfolk erected on a broad field some distance from the keep. As the event neared, jongleurs and acrobats and traveling musicians appeared, hoping to pocket coins during the feasting and festivities to follow.

As these feverish preparations preceded apace, it soon became apparent that Eleanor's gift to Father Anselem had resulted in unintended consequences. The good priest had taken the ruby to the goldsmith's to be assessed and sold for alms to distribute to the poor. Apparently word of its value had spread, and with each telling so had the size and value of Eleanor's dowry. As a result, many more knights than Hugh had originally anticipated sent word that they planned to compete in the tournament.

He also received a letter, delivered by a royal herald, informing him that Queen Eleanor's progress would take her to Oxford and thence to Chester. If her time and energies allowed it, she would detour to Exmoor and attend the festivities honoring Lady Catherine on her name day.

"Her energies?" Lady Alice exclaimed when her son relayed the news. "Ha! She may have passed her seventieth year, but we can't forget this woman accompanied her first husband on

Crusade and presented her second with a quiver-full of ungrateful sons. One of whom now bleeds England dry so he, too, may go on Crusade." Worry creased her forehead. "You must keep *our* Eleanor out of her clutches, Hugh."

"I intend to."

A visit from the queen was still in question when the other guests began to arrive. The bailey rang with the clatter of hooves and shouted instructions to squires and grooms. The knights Hugh had specifically invited would be housed in the keep, their squires and servants in various outbuildings. Sir Giles had assigned the additional combatants to temporary quarters in the village or in tents pitched near the tourney field.

When William Marshal clattered across the drawbridge at the head of an assortment of knights, Hugh and his family hurried out to welcome him. Marshal dismounted and greeted his former squire by ploughing a gloved fist into his shoulder. Hugh managed not to stagger and stood aside for the warrior to greet his mother.

"Sweet Alice!" Wrapping an arm around her waist, Marshal lifted her off her feet and bussed her loudly on both cheeks. "It still pains me that you wed before I could return from Aquitaine and pay proper court to you."

"As I recall," she retorted, laughing, "you were too busy winning tourney prizes and writing songs to Aquitaine's fair duchess to pay court anyone else."

"True, and much good all that wooing did me." Chuckling, he set her on her feet and shot a question at Hugh. "Does she come? The queen?"

"We've not heard for certain, although all is in readiness if she does."

Nodding, Marshal turned his fierce hawk's eyes on Catherine. The girl paled but to Hugh's relief stood her ground as Marshal gripped her outstretched hand and lifted it to his lips.

"My heartiest wishes for the sun to shine bright on your name day, Lady Catherine. If you don't care to bestow your token on this ugly bait-bear you're betrothed to, I'd be honored to wear it in the lists."

Blushing, she stammered her thanks. "I… I would be honored, Sir William, but I've already promised my silk to Hugh." She hesitated, then threw a glance to the woman standing a few paces away. "Mayhap you would carry Lady Eleanor de Brac's favor. She's but newly come from Outremer and as yet has no knight to represent her in the lists."

"De Brac?" The knight's bushy gray brows beetled as his gaze fastened on Eleanor. "I once battled a knight named Simon de Brac in a tourney. At Fougères, I think. Or Chinon. Damned if the rouge didn't come near to unseating me in the last charge of the melee. Are you kin to him?"

She dipped her head in a smiling nod. "He was my father."

Marshal was too chivalrous to voice surprise that such a young and comely maid had sprung from the loins of a man even older and more battle scarred than he was. But Hugh could see his gaze track swiftly from her face to her breasts to the slender handspan of her waist and back again. With the hot summer breeze lifting the ends of her veil to show her coppery hair, she must resemble the duchess he'd wooed so long ago. The Mashal confirmed as much when he took her hand and lifted it to his lips with the grace of a seasoned courtier.

"You look much like the queen you're named for, lady."

"Nay, sir. I'm told she is a great beauty."

"She was when I courted her. Most assuredly, she was."

The Marshal wasn't the only man Eleanor captivated, Hugh noted. A familiar face snagged his glance, and he cursed when he saw Baron Penhammond's dark eyes all but devouring Eleanor where she stood.

"How did your rouge of a father die?" Marshal wanted to know.

"In battle, sir, in Outremer." A small smile played about her lips. "But you may be sure, I've heard the details of that ferocious melee you just described more than once."

"Aye," he snorted, laughing, "I'll warrant you have. So you must give me my revenge and allow me to wear your colors in the lists."

"Or allow me, lady."

As Eleanor turned to Penhammond, Hugh couldn't help but think the snarling wolf's head on the baron's silver-gray surcoat matched the predatory glint in his eyes. A smile cut the saturnine line of his face as he executed a graceful bow and made himself known to Eleanor.

"Allow me to present myself, lady. I am John Powrys, Baron Penhammond. If the rumors are arright, you are in search of a husband. And I, as it chances, am in search of a wife."

Laughing at the blunt declaration, Eleanor gave him her hand. "Then we shall see, baron, whether chance favors the bold."

Dinner that night was a loud, raucous affair. Lady Alice smiled from her seat at the high table but maintained a fierce internal count as course followed course. Stewards, squires, and pages kept the wine and ale flowing. Potential competitors in the lists waved hunks of venison or turkey legs dripping grease while shouting good natured insults across the boards. Acrobats entertained between the courses, and dogs fought over the bones tossed into the rushes.

Some of the clamor died when the troubadour Hugh had summoned for the occasion signaled to his accompanist. When the boy lifted his flute, the high, fluttering notes turned heads and stilled enough noise for the troubadour's baritone to resonate through the great hall as he approached the high table.

"I'm told tomorrow is your name day, Lady Catherine."

"Aye," she whispered, blushing a fiery red as he tugged off his silk cap and swept her a deep bow.

"At the request of Sir Hugh, I sing this poem in your honor."

The *chanson* lasted for at least forty stanzas, but to Eleanor's mind was nowhere near as fanciful or poetic as the songs of the East. She was seated at the high table between Sir Giles and the Marshal. Her position, thankfully, allowed her keep a close eye on Jasmine, seated at a lower table with the other young maids. Relieved that the girl seemed to be behaving herself, Eleanor relaxed a bit and let her gaze roam the hall.

A bold stare caught hers in mid-sweep. It trapped her, held her, refused to release her. Amused, she returned Penhammond's unwavering regard. The baron was nothing if not sure of himself. He'd made his intentions plain enough when he'd arrived. Since that abrupt declaration, Eleanor had made discreet inquires among Lady Alice and her kinswomen. She knew Penhammond had holdings close to the border with Wales. That his villeins barely scratched enough from of his estates to keep him in scutage. That he was unsure which way the wind would blow and had not as yet declared for Richard.

She had to admit the man was as handsome as sin. Well muscled. Clean shaven, with no stink of the stables. And, as she'd learned from her casual inquiries, quite virile. He'd fathered a number of bastards and four legitimate children before losing his wife to the wasting sickness. Now he wanted a second and appeared to have fixed his sights on Eleanor.

What would he would do if she spilled a fortune in rubies into his palm? Would he value her for what she brought him? Or wed her, claim her dower as his, and use her with casual disdain? Eleanor suspected he would certainly try to. So mayhap the more proper question was whether she could manage him as skillfully as she'd managed her father.

She tipped her head and let her lips curve as she considered the matter. He caught the smile, hiked a dark brow, and returned it.

So she wasn't surprised when he made straight for her once the boards were taken down and the floor cleared for dancing. Before he could reach her, however, a slender youth with the face of an angel filled her vision. His eyes were a perfect, guileless blue and his hair haloed his head in a riot of soft gold curls.

"I know I presume, lady, but will you partner me in the ronde?"

"I would be honored, sir, but you must forgive me. I cannot recall your name."

"Harald," he supplied with a smile that lit up his handsome face. "Harald of Broadfields."

She laid her hand lightly on his arm as he led her to the circles forming in the center of the hall. Although the lad was slight and slender, the muscles below the thread-worn silk were as hard as forged steel.

"Have you come to compete in the tourney, Sir Harald?"

"Aye, lady, and to win your hand."

Sweet Mary! He couldn't be much older than Thomas Beckwith, Hugh's squire! But his temperament, Eleanor discovered as the music began and the steps of the dance brought them close, then apart, was far sweeter. He had a simple directness about him that delighted her, particularly when he confessed that he was the fourth of six sons and had made his way in the world on the strength of his arm.

"I've not much to offer a lady such as you," he admitted cheerfully. "But I promise to hold you in great esteem and not beat you without undue provocation."

"That's certainly good to know."

"My father told me to make that point especially," he confided. "And I..."

He broke off, his steps faltering, and gaped at something just over Eleanor's shoulder. She flicked a quick glance behind her and saw that the movement of the circle had brought them directly opposite Hugh and Catherine. The girl's eyes were wide and fixed on Harald. He, for his part, seemed utterly enthralled by the vision across him.

A sudden heaviness dragged at Eleanor's spirit as she gave her partner's hand a discreet tug to get him moving again. If this were a tale from the Arabian Nights, a turbaned genie would spring from a brass lamp and match gentle, timorous Catherine with handsome young Harald. And Eleanor would sit cross-legged on a flying carpet with Hugh and soar across a star-filled sky to a private bower strewn with rose petals.

But this wasn't a fable. Nor an exotic tale of silken sheets and perfumed nights. Catherine belonged to Hugh, and Eleanor to...whomever. The thought put a hard lump in her throat, but the look she gave her unsuspecting partner was so sparkling that he blinked and missed his steps again.

She smothered a sigh of relief when the ronde ended. As sweet as he was, the young knight was hardly a graceful dancer. He'd trod on her toes twice but apologized so profusely that she forgave him instantly. Still, she couldn't help responding to Penhammond's request to partner her in the next dance with a smile that promised more than she intended.

Eleanor realized her mistake too late. By then, the baron had convinced her to escape the hot, crowded hall and take a stroll in the gardens. A full moon lit the graveled paths. The scent of verbena and roses drifted on the humid night air. The sliding trill of a nightingale trying to attract a mate provided a musical chorus as Penhammond guided her through the ornamental box hedge.

Her hand lay lightly on his forearm, as it had on Harald's, and the underlying muscle was every bit as hard and unyielding.

"You'd tire of a pup like Broadfields in a sennight," he said, amusement lacing his voice. "You'd do better to take a husband with some experience of the world."

"One who would keep me on my toes?"

"Nay, lady." He caught her elbow and tugged her around to face him. "One who would keep you on your back."

His bold speaking had amused her earlier. But this went beyond bold and gave Eleanor a swift dislike of him. Or mayhap it was the way his gaze traveled down her body. As if he unlaced her bliaut and stripped off her linen shift where she stood.

Disgusted, she tried to free her arm. "Such vulgarity does you no credit. Release me."

"Not yet," he answered lazily, tightening his grip. "I would have a taste of you, lady, and give you a taste of what you'd get from me."

When he bent his head and covered her mouth with his, she refused to afford him the satisfaction of a struggle. He was too strong and too intent on demonstrating his prowess. Yet she was never more glad of anything in her life when a sardonic drawl cut through the night air.

"Do you think to claim the prize before you win it, Penhammond?"

The baron broke the kiss and raised his head. "The lady raises no objection, Exmoor. Why should you?"

"Because she's under my roof and my protection."

"Only until such time as she leaves both."

"And until that time, you'll keep your hands off her."

Exmoor's cool reply carried a warning that raised the fine hairs on Eleanor's nape. The baron heard the underlying threat, as well, and for a moment his grip tightened even more. Then he released her and sketched a sardonic bow.

"My apologies for the interruption, lady. Next time I'll ensure we have more privacy."

Gravel crunched under his feet as he strolled back through the moonlit garden. Mortified at having let herself be maneuvered into such an embarrassing situation, Eleanor tried to come up with an explanation that didn't sound paltry, even to herself. She was still floundering when Exmoor's icy disdain cut into her like a whip.

"You would be wise to refrain from enticing other suitors to sample your charms. Such conduct might give the more honorable among them a disgust of you."

The rebuke stung, all the more because she knew it was well deserved. But sheer perversity lifted her chin. "I thank you for your concern, sir. But I'm well able to take the measure of any suitors."

Her defiant reply seemed to break the hold he had on his temper. His nostrils flared, and even in the filtered light of the moon Eleanor could see the anger that leaped into his eyes as he stalked toward her.

"Hear me, lady, and hear me well. As long as you are in my keeping, you will conduct yourself as befits a woman of my household. You will not taunt with seductive smiles and smoldering glances, or allow a man to put his hands on you and use you like a common whore."

The fact that she'd done just that took none of the outrage from her gasp. Furious, she stood toe to toe with him. "How righteous you are. How upright and indignant. Have you never kissed a maid in a moonlit garden?"

"Don't play the fool. You know the rules are different for men."

The truth of that only fired her resentment. "Oh, so? Then I must make sure to choose a suitor who'll act with more restraint. That handsome young knight with the eyes of poet, mayhap? Harald of Broadfields? I'm sure I can trust myself and my honor with him."

The taunt stroked the anger she saw in Exmoor's face. "You'd best not torment or tease that stripling. He's not man enough to handle you."

"Ah, now we come to it." Her fists went to her hips. Her lips pulled back in a sneer. "And who, milord, do you consider man enough for me? Not Broadfields. Nor Penhammond, it appears. You'd best give me a list of names, so I know who to throw out lures to."

She knew she was baiting a chained bear. And her heart burst into a wild song when he broke those chains.

Wrapping a fist around her upper arm, he dragged her deeper into the shadows. Her shoulders hit the stone wall. His hand circled her throat, forcing her chin up and her head back.

"If you will play the whore, play it with me."

Merciful Mother of God! She'd ached for this! His mouth was hungry on hers. His muscles taut where they pressed into her. She flattened her palms against stone still warm from the heat of the day and felt him rise hard and rampant against her belly.

She felt no shame. No vestige of doubt. Only a woman's need that burst deep inside her. So strong, it arched her back and canted her hips into his. So fierce, she could scarce breathe for the force of it.

His need was no less savage. He cupped her breast, his palm hard through her layers of shift and gown, and kneaded the taut flesh. She felt her nipple peak under the rough handling and ached for more.

So much more, that she didn't protest when he forced a knee between hers. His thigh was like an iron bar, prizing hers apart, near lifting her off her feet. All the while his mouth ravaged hers.

Her body responded with instincts older than time. Heat spiraled through her. Her most private places went tight, then wet. A need built within her that begged for release. Desperate but unsure how to bring that release about, she dug her hands into his shoulders and rode him as she would Sirocco.

Sensations she'd never experienced, much less imagined, drew her as taut a bowstring. The feeling was frightening in its intensity. So frightening she tried to wiggle free. He held her place, his breath coming as fast and harsh as hers.

"Hugh!"

It was a cry. A mindless plea. It burst from her as a wild tide crashed over her, flooding her belly, rushing up through her chest, closing her throat. Groaning, she clung to him to keep from drowning.

Slowly, so slowly, her senses stopped spinning. Just as slowly, she dragged her head up. She couldn't speak. No words could describe what she'd just experienced.

It was left to Hugh to break the silence. When he did, his voice was low and raw with self-disgust. "Forgive me, Elenor. The fault for this lays on me, and me alone."

Somehow she found the strength for a weak chuckle. "I suspect Father Anselem might argue that point."

"He might, until I confessed that I was racked by jealousy when I saw you depart the hall on Penhammond's arm. I followed you apurpose, mayhap with just such as this in mind."

"Oh, Hugh." Her breath left on a ragged sigh. "The evil demon of jealousy has bitten me, too. I love Catherine. Truly, I do. She's sweet and gentle and so generous of heart. Yet when I saw you partnering her in the dance tonight, I wanted to…to…"

"Exact a measure of revenge by allowing Penhammond to take you into the garden?"

"Aye."

There! They'd acknowledged the truth at last. The hunger that that went against the laws of God and man. It wracked them both, yet Exmoor insisted on shouldering the blame.

"The sin is mine," he said again. "I goaded you into anger. Then I responded to your fury by backing you against this wall and coming as close as no matter to dishonoring you."

"As close as no matter? I may be a maid, but I've heard enough from married women to know that was *not* as close as it could have been."

He gave a reluctant laugh and laid his forehead against hers. "Ah, Eleanor."

She was still in thrall to that dark pleasure… That wild release…

Confused beyond measure, she edged away from him. Her disordered robe dropped back into respectable folds but her hair would require the attentions of a maid before she showed herself in the great hall again.

Just as well. She needed time to calm her chaotic thoughts and soothe the growing ache in her heart. Acknowledging their hunger for each other had solved nothing, she now realized. And the hot, searing pleasure his hands and mouth had given her had only added to her guilt.

"Confess what you will to Father Anselem," she told him softly. "You will follow your conscience, as I will mine. And now I must retire and right my hair or my suitors will, indeed, think me the wanton."

Hugh let her go, his gaze on the silvery shimmer of her veil as it fluttered in the moonlight. Only when she'd disappeared around the corner tower did he unclench his fists. He had no ear for the warbling nightingales. No consciousness of the roses and moonflowers that scented the air. Eleanor still filled his mind, his senses.

She could never know how close he'd come to dragging up her skirts and thrusting into her. How savagely he'd ached to spill his seed in her wet, welcoming heat. Even now, the mere thought made his belly roll and his groin knot.

God alone knew how he'd held back! He must've felt some tug of sanity. Some bite of conscience. But whatever his reason for restraint when he'd had Eleanor so willing and eager escaped him now. All he could think of, all his mind could see, was her head thrown back. Her slender neck arched. Her breasts pushing against her bodice as she gasped and groaned out her pleasure.

Still shaken, he hammered his fist against his thigh. Had he lost all honor? Was he ready to debase himself for a pair of sparkling eyes and a laugh that drove him to distraction? As much as he desired Eleanor de Brac, he couldn't have her.

Unless…

No! He couldn't break his vow and send Catherine back to her father. The girl might quake like a trapped doe whenever Hugh came within a few feet of her, but she feared her father far more than she did him.

His betrothal vows sat like a millstone on his shoulders as he made his way through the shadowed garden. He muttered a fervent prayer of thanks to God that the weather had held and the tournament would begin as scheduled tomorrow. It would start with jousts, which seasoned combatants generally left to the younger, more impecunious knights.

But then would come the melee, a neck-for-nothing charge of heavily armed and armored warriors. Axes swinging. Swords flashing. Shields crashing into shields. Blood and sweat and screams.

Exactly, Hugh thought viciously, what he craved!

Chapter Nine

Hugh woke at dawn the next morning in a foul mood. He'd slept little. His hunger for Eleanor and his disgust with himself for coming so close to dishonoring them both had gnawed at his conscience through most of the night.

His duties as host forced him to maintain a pleasant mien but he could feel his gorge rise when he caught Penhammond's sardonic glance or saw that young fool Harald hovering like a great gawk at Eleanor's shoulder. She, too, looked as though she'd slept poorly. Her smile was as ready as always, but to Hugh's critical eye it lacked its usual warmth. She even chastised Jasmine with surprising sharpness when the girl came late to Mass. Jasmine took the reprimand with a mulish set to her lips that warned all who knew her to beware.

A display of temper from that imp would be all he needed to sour his mood even more, Hugh thought grimly. The elder sister had best keep the younger on a short rein during the tourney. With that in mind, he drew Eleanor into a shallow alcove as they descended the stairs on their way to the great hall to break their fast.

"Have an eye to your sister for the next few days," he warned. "Given her penchant for tumbling into mischief, she's like as not to set fire to one of the tents or get caught in the middle of the melee."

"I'll do my best," she promised tersely.

Hugh hesitated, knowing they should speak of last night but strangely loathe to bring those stolen moments into the harsh light of day.

Eleanor showed no such restraint. "I spent much of the night thinking about what happened in the garden," she murmured, her words for him alone as others edged their way past them on their way to the great hall. "We neither of us have aught to confess. You held to your vows to Catherine, and I will hold to mine to take a husband and rid you of the temptation of my presence."

Looking down into the face that now filled his dreams, he came within a hair's breadth of saying to the devil with his vows! Declaring on the instant that he would foreswear himself for her if she would...

"Ah, Catherine!" Eleanor's emerald gaze fixed on a presence behind him, and a forced smile lightened her countenance. "There you are. I searched for you in the ladies bower when I awoke this morning, but you had already gone down to prayers."

Hugh turned to see his betrothed descend the stairs toward them. She gave them both a hesitant glance.

"Did you...? Did you wish to speak with me, Eleanor?"

"Yes, and to give you this in honor of your name day."

Eleanor loosened the drawstring pouch hanging from her girdle and withdrew a small fold of some shiny material. With a twitch of her wrist, she flipped the folds open to reveal a much larger square of shimmering pink silk shot with silver threads.

"Lady Alice told me that you plan to wear your new rose-dyed gown to the tourney." Her smile turned teasing. "Should you wish it, you could allow your chosen champion to carry this silk in the lists."

"I...ah..."

Hugh took pity on the fiery blush that stained her cheeks. "Catherine knows I don't ride in the lists. I leave that to the younger, hungrier knights. She may award her favor to one of them, if she's see fit."

While Catherine fumbled for a reply, Jasmine rushed up the stairs and demanded her sister's attention.

"Eleanor! Come and break your fast! Then we must go watch the barding of the knights." Her eyes shone with excitement. "Guy says he's to help your squire, Hugh."

"Aye, and so he is."

Which, Hugh had decided, was as good a way of any to keep the lad from being led into mischief by this eager sprite. Or so he hoped.

"Guy said that Sirocco's barding is the finest of all." The girl danced from foot to foot in her impatience. "You'll want to see that, Eleanor! Come, we need to get to the stables."

"Jasmine! Don't you have something to give Catherine first?"

"Oh! Aye." Squirming with impatience, she dug into the pouch attached to the belt girding her girlish hips and drew out a small vial. "This is sand from the Holy Land, lady. May it comfort you when you say your prayers."

"Oh, Jasmine!" Catherine's face suffused with joy. "Thank you!" She clasped the vial to her bosom. "I could not ask for a greater gift."

"Yes, yes." Jasmine turned an imploring glance on her sister. "Can we go now?"

With an exasperated laugh, Eleanor kissed Catherine's cheek, wished her joy on her name day and trailed her skipping sister toward the stairs. Catherine would have followed but Hugh caught her elbow.

"Wait, Cat."

She hesitated, looking for all the world like a trapped deer. "Yes, my lord?"

Hugh battled a familiar irritation while the ill humor that had dogged him since he'd rolled out of bed pricked at him once again. "I, too, have a gift for you in honor of your name day."

Surprise filled her heart-shaped face as he slipped a hammered silver bracelet studded with garnets and pearls onto her wrist. Stammering, she lifted her eyes to his.

"It's... It's beautiful, my lord. I thank you."

She gave him a brave smile and for once didn't shrink away when he bent to brush a kiss across her lips. For some reason, her display of courage only added to Hugh's uncertain temper.

"You're welcome. Now come and eat, so you don't faint away during the lists."

The order came out more gruffly than he'd intended, and Hugh swallowed a curse when her smile faded.

"I'll join you shortly," she promised, her eyes downcast. "But first I….I must give thanks to the Lord for this, my name day."

"As you will."

Shrinking back into the alcove, Catherine watched her lord descend the stone stairs. She'd thought herself miserable before. Too frightened to be a wife to her husband, ashamed of her fears, yet unable to banish them. She could hardly bear to meet Lady Alice's glance any more.

But this…! This misery was almost more than she could bear!

She might be timorous, but she wasn't slow-witted. Nor was she blind. Eleanor de Brac had fascinated Hugh since the day she'd galloped into their lives. And why would she not? The vibrant, flame-haired beauty was everything Catherine was not. Bold and merry and not the least afeared to stand her ground. It didn't take a magician or one of Jasmine's fantastical jinnis to see that Hugh became a different man in Eleanor's presence. More sardonic, to be sure, but with a glint in his eyes that only she seemed to spark. That look was so different from the deliberate patience that suffused his face when he dealt with his betrothed that Catherine couldn't hold back a sob.

To smother it, she buried her face in the sparkling cloth Eleanor had gifted her with. Hugh would hold to his betrothal vows, she knew. And she to hers. The pain that inescapable fact pierced her heart and…

"M'lady?"

She shrank against the stone wall, keeping her face hidden.

"Lady Catherine, I beg you! Allow me to help if I can."

She lowered the cloth and felt her heart bump inside her chest. The knight was so young and so handsome and so very distressed by her tears.

"I… I thank you, Sir Harald." Gulping, she struggled for an explanation that wouldn't completely shame her. "I'm but… but overcome by the gifts bestowed on me in honor of my name day." Summoning a watery smile, she held out an arm. "My lord gave me this bracelet. Lady Eleanor, this beautiful veil, and little Jasmine a vial with sand from the Holy Land."

Instead of admiring her gifts, the young knight muttered a fierce declaration. "Would that I, too, had a gift to give you."

As his eyes burned into hers, Catherine's heart gave another queer little thump.

"Alas, I have not," he confessed. "Except to honor you in the lists. If you will let me wear your token, that is."

Uncertainty pulsed through Catherine's veins. She'd never been feted at a tournament before, much less had a knight beg to carry her token. As quickly as it had come, however, the girlish happiness fled.

"You must carry Lady Eleanor's token! She's the prize you've come to win, is she not?"

"She is. And win her I will. But…"

For one breathless moment Catherine thought he would reach for her. That she would not tremble under his kiss, as she did Hugh's. Then the fear that held her very soul in thrall made her shrink back against the wall.

Harald could not but note her reaction. Disappointment clouded his handsome face but he merely bowed, wished her a happy name day, and said he hoped to see her at the tourney.

The keep's residents and guests broke their fast with slabs of bread, boiled beef and honeyed oats. Sir Giles, whose reddened eyes and bristly chin suggested he'd slept but little the night before, sent baskets of meats and fresh bread to the lesser knights and squires who'd bedded down in tents near the field.

A fever of anticipation gripped the entire keep as the sun climbed over the battlements and the knights assembled in the bailey so their squires could outfit and mount them. The scene was one of great noise, color, and movement. Chickens squawked and pigs squealed as they dodged boots and hooves. War horses bred for battle stamped their massive hooves and snorted challenges to each other as grooms held them in rigid check. Pennants and surcoats and barding boasted rich embroidery and distinctive emblems.

Since he wasn't participating in the lists, Hugh would ride Sirocco to the field. Guy's chest was puffed with pride as he grasped bridle to lead the courser out of the stables.

"Don't jerk his head so!" Jasmine admonished from her perch on a wooden wheelbarrow.

Guy threw her an impatient glance. Like him, she was dressed in her finest garb for the occasion. Her silky black hair was unbound and spilled freely down her back as befitted a girl of her tender years. Lavishly embroidered birds and flowers decorated the hem and square neck of her forest-green bliaut, and the toes of her red leather shoes curled back on themselves.

"You've no business in the stables," he told her as Sirocco blew a hot breath at the back of his neck. "You'll dirty your gown."

"Pah! Do I care for such matters?"

"No, but you should! This tourney is as much for Eleanor's benefit as it is to honor Catherine. You'll not do either of them honor by appearing at the lists with muck on your skirts and smelling of the stables."

His admonition didn't sit well with his young companion. Irritated, she made a crude comment regarding Guy's self-important air and peacock finery. He ignored her and led Sirocco into the bailey.

As Hugh had anticipated, the Arabian courser caused a chorus of exclamations. One knight in particular seemed taken with the steed's powerful lines. Edging his own mount close enough to earn a warning snort from Sirocco, he ran approving eyes from withers to haunches.

"I'd heard talk at Chester about this destrier, Exmoor. Where did you acquire him?"

Hugh knew the man only slightly. The bastard get of an earl, Ian FitzGilbert had sold his sword to the highest bidder almost before he could wield it. He now wore the proof of many battles in the scar that cut across one cheek and a nose that looked as though it had taken the full brunt of a heavily embossed shield. FitzGilbert had arrived in William Marshall's entourage and been seated well below the salt at the banquet last night. Despite his fearsome appearance, however, he had a reputation for treating captives honorably, his deceased wife gently, and his three children with gruff affection.

What's more, Hugh guessed FitzGilbert had yet to see his thirtieth year. He was still relatively young. And strong. And virile, judging by his youthful brood. The precise requirements Eleanor desired in a husband.

Fighting to smother a sudden and inexplicable dislike for the battle-scarred warrior, Hugh replied with forced politeness. "He was a gift."

"From the Lady Eleanor," Guy put in as his brother swung from the mounting block into the saddle. Eager to tout Sirocco's powers, he missed Hugh's frown. "She named him for the winds that race across the desert."

"Oh, so?"

FitzGilbert raked the magnificent mount with another glance before lifting his frost-gray eyes to its rider. "So the rumors are true? In addition to the manor and the silver you've dowered the lady with, she brings treasures of her own from the East?"

"I'll discuss her dower with the man who wins her," Hugh answered cooly, "and none other."

"Then I must be sure to win her," FitzGilbert replied with a crooked smile. His glance flicked to Penhammond, currently mounting his own warhorse, and the smile faded. "A contest to look forward to," he said with soft but unmistakable menace.

The murmur drew a sharp glance from Hugh but before he could probe the reason for it, the door to the keep opened and Lady Alice led out a laughing, chattering troop of ladies. Their jeweled circlets and necklets and girdles flashed a rainbow of dazzling colors. Hugh smiled fondly at his mother, who looked far younger than her years in a gown of Exmoor blue. Catherine wore her new gown, as well. The deep rose color showed her to great advantage, and when the Marshal told her so, she blushed an ever deeper pink.

But Eleanor...!

God's bones, Eleanor!

She'd chosen a gown that echoed the shades of a fiery sunset. With each step, the exotic fabric gave off glints of gold and rose and flaming scarlet. The veil covering her hair was the sheerest, almost translucent silk. The circlet anchoring it in place was a modest braid of woven gold threads, though. Hugh couldn't help but think how it should be a band of hammered gold studded with her magnificent rubies.

As vivid as her present image was, he could not but help remember how she looked in the garden last night. Her face turned to his. Her eyes dark with passion. Her mouth swollen from his kiss. The memory caused a now familiar twist to his gut as he saluted the ladies and waited while they dispersed to their chosen conveyances.

Lady Alice had disdained the waiting litters, indicating she would ride to the field. So would Catherine and Eleanor and most of the younger women. Including Jasmine, Hugh noted with a fervent prayer that the girl could keep her palfrey in check. He needn't have worried. Once mounted, the younger sister handled the reins with same ease as the elder.

At last they were ready to depart. A groom led Catherine's docile mare forward so she could take her place beside Hugh. William Marshal claimed the honor of riding next to Lady Alice, who blushed like a girl at his outrageous compliments. When the rest formed into colorful cortège, Hugh noted that FitzGilbert had managed to position himself next to Eleanor. The adroit maneuver earned him a frown from young Harald of Broadfields and a narrow-eyed stare from Penhammond. None of the three men were worthy of her, Hugh thought grimly. And the very real possibility that she might choose one of them kept his jaw tight as he led the procession across the wooden drawbridge.

Pennants flying, silks fluttering, armor clinking and flashing in the sunlight, they made a brave sight. Most of the residents of the village at the base of the steep incline had already made their way to the tourney field. The few that remained came out of their huts to cheer and shout well wishes to their lord and the knights wearing his colors.

A raucous crowd had already gathered at the tourney site. After tomorrow's melee, the field would be a sea of mud plowed up by pawing hooves and desperately battling knights. On this bright summer morning, however, the site had the color and festive atmosphere of a fair. Hastily erected booths offered everything from hot pasties to palm reading. Jugglers and musicians strolled the grounds. The disciplined rows of tents Sir Giles had erected for the lesser knights and their squires buzzed with activity.

Hugh led the way to the gaily striped tent shading the viewing stand. Dismounting, he waved his squire aside and lifted Catherine from the saddle himself. William Marshall did the same for Lady Alice but young Harald was at Eleanor's side before either FitzGilbert or Penhammond could dismount. Belying his slender frame, Broadfields lifted her easily and set her on her feet, before dropping to one knee.

Even Hugh, watching with a sardonic smile, had to admit that the young knight exhibited a grace and gallantry that songs were sung of as he begged a token.

"Would you give me your favor to carry in the lists, lady?"

The crowd that had followed the procession to the stands signaled their approval by stamping and clapping.

"I would, Sir Harald, and gladly," Eleanor said with a smile. "But…"

Penhammond took a step toward her. She ignored him, however, and turned to the knight who'd escorted her.

"I've already promised it to Sir Ian."

Young Harald took the loss with a good natured shrug. He pushed to his feet, and only those closest to him saw his gaze drift from Eleanor to Catherine. And only someone who'd come to know his betrothed as well as Hugh had could spot the confusion in her eyes as she gazed on him.

For pity's sake! The lad was besotted with her. Yet she could not accept even his worshipful adoration. Hugh only needed that to set the seal to his temper as Eleanor withdrew a square of shimmering silk from her sleeve. FitzGilbert tied the favor to the spike of his helm. Then he bowed and kissed her hand just as the trumpeter hired especially for the event signaled its start.

Since Hugh had chosen not participate in the joust, he joined his family, William Marshall, Sir Giles and his wife, and various other guests and members of his household in the stands to watch. The trumpet called the first combatants. Hugh knew one knight and recognized the other from the device on his shield. He leaned down to identify them to Catherine as they took their places at either end of the run.

Lances were set into *arrets* to steady them. Visors clanked down. Sensing their riders' tension, their mounts shied, pawed the ground, and rolled their eyes behind their protective face armor while squires stood ready with spare lances. Normally, each knight would run four courses, but given the number who'd signaled their desire to participate, Sir Giles had shortened it to three.

The first contest ended after the second run. Both knights splintered their lances but only one went down when his mount took full brunt of the hit. The fallen knight, Hugh explained, was the winner since the fault was with his horse and not him.

"That's hardly fair!" Catherine exclaimed, her soft heart wrung by the sight of the injured warhorse struggling to rise.

"Fair or not, a knight afoot is at a grievous disadvantage. Hence he's given the win in the joust. You'll find it's a vastly different matter in the melee."

The brutal truth of that was brought home the next morning.

The combatants charged at each other across a wide swath of open field, slashing and hacking in close quarters before they wheeled and charged again. Swords battered shields. Axes clanged against blades. Shouts and taunts and groans carried across the air. For this contest, Exmoor rode a war horse with powerful flanks and a massive chest. The beast didn't have Sirocco's speed nor, Eleanor guessed, his endurance. But he looked to be a battering ram on the hoof.

"Hell and damnation." She pushed up on tiptoe after the first charge. "Can you see who's still ahorse?"

"No," Catherine whispered, gulping. The brutality of the melee had raised her gorge.

These were war-trained knights, she knew. Out to prove their mettle and add to their reputations. Out also, to claim rich prizes in ransom. Their shouts echoed with glee and bravado and grim determination, but Catherine could only imagine the worst. What if Hugh was injured? What if he died? Both happened in melees. All too frequently, she'd been told. Then what would become of her? She couldn't go back to her father with his ready fists and bruised, sobbing wife. She couldn't!

"I can't see a thing." Eleanor complained. "Come with me, Catherine."

Before Lady Alice realized their intent, the two were out of the stands. Skirts lifted, they raced for the hillock crowded with villeins watching and wagering on the various combatants. Jasmine followed in close pursuit. When the girl caught up with her sister, Eleanor grabbed her hand and held it tight as they plunged through the throng of excited watchers.

The air reeked with sweat and onions and fish stew. Feet stomped. Huzzah's filled the air. The watchers' excitement added to Eleanor's as she and Catherine and Jasmine worked their way to a spot with a clear view of the field.

"He's still ahorse!" Eleanor exclaimed when she spotted a familiar golden eagle on a field of blue.

"No," Catherine countered on a gasp, "he's not."

Eleanor started to point to Exmoor, well in the thick of things, when she realized that the younger woman's horrified gaze was fixed on a knight struggling to regain his feet while fighting off a determined attacker. Then she, too, held her breath as young Harald parried several crippling blows with his shield.

"He should yield!" Catherine's fingers dug into Eleanor's arm. "Why doesn't he yield?"

Wincing, Eleanor tried to ease her arm from the younger woman's grip as another knight leaped into the fray. A stunning blow from the flat of his sword felled Harald's attacker. He crumpled, obviously stunned, then held up both gloved hands. The newcomer took his surrender with a jerk of his chin, then whirled and thrust the tip of his spear at Harald's throat. Eleanor gasped, loathe to see her young swain hurt, then sagged in relief when he raised a hand in surrender.

"Can you see who bested him?" Catherine asked, still shaken by the brutality of the melee.

Eleanor squinted into the distance. The victor was too mud-spattered for her to discern either the barding or surcoat, but she did recognize the now-limp square of silk tied to his helm.

"It's Ian FitzGilbert."

"FitzGilbert? *He* took down Harald? But he's so…so old!"

"Not *that* old" Eleanor returned dryly, her mind already made up as to who she would take to husband.

Chapter Ten

The ladies rode back to the keep while victor and vanquished remained on the field to negotiate ransoms. Such deliberations, Lady Alice informed the others, could take hours. In the meantime, the women had much to do. There was water to be heated for baths, medicines and bandages to be readied, additional tuns of wine and ale to be rolled out for combatants and spectators alike, and the boards to be laid for the final banquet.

Once back at the keep, Lady Alice dismounted with more haste than grace. Before hurrying to the sheds to check on her small army of cooks and kitchen helpers, she issued a barrage of instructions. "Lady Margaret, please see that the ointments and rolls of lint we laid out in readiness are brought to the yard."

"I'll attend to it now," Sir Gile's wife promised. "But we'll need more comfy for poultices. We've ground every leaf from the garden into powder."

"Comfy springs up like weed. There are patches growing wild along the river bank. Send someone to gather a basketful. But be sure they can tell it from baneberry, else the men will be emptying their bowels while we try to knit their bones!"

"I'll go," Catherine offered. "I picked the last of the comfy in the garden. I know its leaves well."

"Good. Take an escort with you."

"I will."

"And you, Eleanor. Would you be so good as to tell Father Anselem that none of the participants appear to have taken a mortal wound. He asked to be advised as soon as possible if he needed to conduct a funeral Mass."

"Of course."

Her mind obviously racing with all that needed to be done, Lady Alice dispersed the women to their various tasks with a flap of her hand and turned toward the kitchen sheds, only to swing back.

"Where's Jasmine?"

Eleanor halted, skimmed a quick glance around the busy inner bailey, and frowned. "She was beside me when we rode up to the gate."

"You'd best find her, and quickly. God only knows what deviltry she'll get into if left to her own devices."

Eleanor couldn't disagree with that tart assessment. Never one for domestic chores if she could avoid them, Jasmine no doubt intended to keep well out of sight until Guy and the men returned.

Eleanor checked the stables, the kennels, the dovecote and the mews but didn't grow unduly alarmed until a search of the hay byre and carp pond failed to produce the girl. She found her at last in the orchard, perched on the sturdy, low-lying branch of her favorite apple tree. She'd kicked off her slippers and hiked up her skirt. Only her bare feet were visible through the screen of leaves, and they swung in jerky little arcs.

"Here you are. I've been looking for you."

"Why?"

"Why would I not? We've much to do, Jasmine, to ready for the banquet."

"*You've* much to do, you mean."

Frowning, Eleanor pushed aside the branches to gain a clearer view of her sister. The girl's arms were folded across her chest and her face was set in an ominous frown.

"What's put you in a temper? You were lively enough on the ride back to the keep."

"I heard them. Lady Alice and Catherine." Chin tucked, she glared at her sister from beneath angry brows. "They said Hugh will announce tonight who you'll take to husband."

"Well…"

"And then we'll leave Exmoor."

"So we will."

"But I don't want to go." The fingers gripping her crossed elbows pressed harder. "I like it here. I like Lady Alice and Guy. Even Father Anselem when he's not trying to wean me from my heathenish ways. Hugh, too, although he displays a *most* foul temper at times."

"Only when you goad him beyond bearing," Eleanor teased. "But…"

She ducked under another branch and leaned her shoulders against the thick bough supporting her sister. Jasmine was nothing if not fierce in her loyalties. She'd adored their ramshackle father and had even, apparently, come to accept Hugh in her life. Small wonder. His handling of the girl disguised a rough affection that neither he nor Jasmine were ready to admit to. Eleanor could only hope the man she took to husband would prove as generous of heart.

The thought of giving herself in marriage stirred a flutter of doubt, quickly supplanted by steely resolve. She'd traveled all the way from Outremer with this one goal in mind. A goal that had quickly became wrapped within others. She couldn't help but think back to her first meeting with Hugh and Catherine all these weeks ago. She'd been so confident, so blithely certain that she could avert what she'd recognized at once was as a misalliance. Yet instead of freeing man and maid from a marriage neither wanted, she'd ensnared them all in a tangled web of desire and deceit.

She lusted for Hugh as much as he did for her. Yet he was sworn to Catherine. Kind, timid, frightened little Catherine. The only solution was for Eleanor to choose a husband and be gone.

"You know we planned to stay at Exmoor only until I found a suitable husband," she reminded Jasmine. "One we could both admire and respect."

"And have you found him?"

"Yes."

"Please say you've not chosen the ferret with the dark eyes and sneer for a smile."

"Penhammond? No."

"That young gawk with the hay-colored hair? He's but a few years older than I am. What's more, he's all muck-eyes over Catherine."

Even Jasmine had noticed? Eleanor would have to drop a word of warning in Catherine's ear.

"No, not Harald."

"Then who?"

"The knight I gave my token to today."

Jasmine's forehead scrunched. "The big one? With the scar?"

"Yes. Lady Alice had told me all about him," she said, trying to decide how much to share. "His holding is small, but he won it with the strength of this arm."

"Is it far from here?"

"I'm not sure."

"Too far for Guy to come to visit?"

"I don't know. But I do know his wife died last year, so he needs a mother for his baby… and a big sister for his other children."

"Like you were for me." Jasmine pursed her lips, considering. "How old are they, these of children of his?"

"Young, Lady Alice said. Younger than you, even."

Jasmine swung her heels as the prospect of being an older sister took root. "I could teach them many things."

With a silent apology to FitzGilbert, Eleanor nodded. "Indeed, you could."

The girl thought about it for a few more moments. "When do we leave?"

"Soon, I would guess. Mayhap even tomorrow. I'll speak to Sir Ian this eve. If we agree we'll suit, he'll no doubt wish to conclude the matter as quickly as possible."

Jasmine blew out a long breath and pushed off the low hanging bough. "I can't promise to like him," she confessed with brutal honesty. "But if he's not kind to you, I *do* promise to put pig slop in his boots and burrs under his saddle."

Her eyes stinging, Eleanor swept her sister into a fierce hug. "I would expect nothing less."

Having cleared that hurdle, there was nothing left for her to do but advise Father Anselem that he needn't prepare a funeral Mass, change her muddied robe, and wait for Hugh to return to the keep.

He clattered across the drawbridge some hours later in the company of a roisterous group that included William Marshal, Sir Giles, and Ian FitzGilbert. Watching from a tower window, Eleanor could see no sign of Baron Penhammond or young Harald. She wasn't surprised at their abrupt departure. The ransoms they would've had to pledge after losing in the melee would make them in no mood to enjoy the victors' jibes and jests at the banquet.

The men dismounted and issued orders to their squires regarding their horses and weapons. Lady Alice would have cauldrons hot water ready for them by the kitchen sheds, as well as a small army of maids and attendants to salve their bruises. Eleanor had offered to help. The good Lord knew she'd tended to her father's bruises and broken bones often enough. But Lady Alice flatly refused, insisting she would allow no unmarried female in her keeping attend to unclothed knights.

Hugh would be among them. Eleanor's agile mind could picture all too vividly his body mottled with bruises from the brutal melee. She ached to wash away his sweat and grime and blood, then soothe his hurts. The chest-piercing intensity of that urge had her turning away from the tower window, thoroughly shamed and doubly resolved to leave Exmoor Keep before she compounded her sins of jealousy and lust for a man she could not have.

Determined to get the task done, she penned a quick note. It galled her to solicit Hugh's approval of her choice but she knew she must obtain it before she informed Ian FitzGilbert that she would have him as husband. The note was stiff and formal and begged Hugh grant her a brief audience. The page who delivered the request returned with a brief note stating that Hugh would meet her in the orchard in an hour's time.

Eleanor spent the interval helping lay the boards and ensuring that the extra tuns of ale Lady Alice had ordered for the feast to come were at hand and ready to be tapped. All the while, the realization that she would in all likelihood say goodbye to this keep and its lord on the morrow sat like a millstone on her heart.

When she saw him waiting for her in the shade of Jasmine's favorite tree, however, she summoned a bright smile. Like her, he'd scrubbed away the muck and mud of the tourney field. His cheeks and chin were pumiced, his blue eyes cautious and waiting.

"So, my lord," she said with a forced gaiety. "I watched you in the melee. You laid about with fearsome strokes. Did you take many ransoms?"

"A goodly enough amount."

"I saw Penhammond yield to you."

A glint of savage satisfaction lit his eyes. "I took his arms and wolf's shield as prize, but left him with his horse so he could slink back to his lair."

"Oh, Hugh!" His words as much as his tone wiped the forced levity from her face. "It shames me that I stirred such enmity between you and Penhammond. From what you say, there's trouble enough brewing in England without a silly, stupid female adding coals to the fire."

His grim expression lightened a bit. "The enmity was there long before a certain silly female fanned the flames."

"If you say so," she answered doubtfully.

"I do."

She hesitated, but couldn't avoid the matter hovering between them like a dark cloud any longer. "I also saw Harald of Broadfields go down."

"Aye. He yielded to FitzGilbert."

"So…" She drew in a long, steadying breath. "FitzGilbert has made plain that he would take me to wife if I'll have him." She paused again, her heart throwing itself against her ribs like a caged beast. "I will, if you have no objection."

No objection.

The words slammed into Hugh like battle-ax swung full force against his helm. For a wild moment he actually considered withholding his consent.

He could foreswear his oath.

End his betrothal.

Send Catherine back to her father

And keep for himself the woman he now craved like a drowning man did air.

Kings put aside wives when and where they wished. Earls and barons switched loyalties with the tides. Hell, even John Pigman had rid himself of his shrew of a wife by proving to Father Anselem that she was, hitherto unbeknownst to him, his first cousin.

The vicious urge to hack through the ties that bound him to Catherine near ripped Hugh apart. But he unclenched his fists and took the only course his conscience allowed.

"I have no objection. FitzGilbert may be base-born, but he's earned both honor and respect. I'll speak to him before we go in to dinner."

A silence fell between them, thick and heavy and broken only by buzz of the bees flitting from blossom to blossom and the faint noises coming from the bailey. They had nothing more to say. Either of them. Yet neither moved…until at last Hugh reached out a hand.

He intended merely to grasp her elbow. Escort her back to the keep. Hand her over to the man who would take her to wife…and to his bed. Ever afterward, he could not say whether he used that light hold to tug her closer or she came into his arms of her own accord.

He was a man grown. He knew well how to govern his passions. But the feel of her against him, the taste of her mouth on his, made a mockery of his hard-learned restraint. Against all reason, against his will, he crushed her against him and took a last farewell.

"Hugh, I'm worried for…. Sweet Mary!"

His mother's exclamation jerked them apart. Lady Alice stood frozen some yards away. Her shocked expression gave way to dismay, then to swift, angry censure.

"I thought better of you, my son. And of you, Eleanor."

Lips tight, she raked them with a look that had Eleanor cringing in shame and Hugh feeling much the same age as Guy. Although it galled him to offer an explanation for his conduct, he knew he would not escape the garden without one.

"Eleanor has decided to take Ian FitzGilbert to husband," he informed his mother coolly. "We were but saying farewell."

"Ha!" Her inelegant snort told him what she thought of his feeble excuse. "If that was farewell, I don't wish to think what came between hello and goodbye."

Hugh stiffened, about to remind her that he was no longer a lad to be scolded, but Eleanor held out a beseeching hand.

"I swear by the Holy Virgin, Lady Alice, we've done naught but share a kiss or…" She stopped, her cheeks flaming almost the same bright red as her hair, then finished weakly. "Two."

Hugh knew she was thinking of how he'd brought her to moaning pleasure with his hands and mouth and knee pressed hard between her thighs. Guilt was writ so plainly across her face that his mother muttered an oath he'd never heard come from her lips before.

Daunted but determined, Eleanor tried again. "I swear on all that's holy. I go to FitzGilbert still a maid, and Hugh has held true to his vows to Catherine."

"Catherine!"

Instant worry replaced the disapproval on Lady Alice's face.

"She's the reason I came to find you, Hugh. I sent her to gather comfy nigh onto three hours ago. She's not returned. I've been so busy I didn't realize it until a few moments past."

He reached his mother's side in a few, swift strides. "Did she take an escort?"

"A maid and two men-at-arms, as best I can discover."

"Do you know which direction they went?"

"I told her to look along the river. Comfy grows in great clumps on its banks."

He headed for the bailey without another word. His mother hurried behind him, as did Eleanor. She hoped against hope that Catherine had but dallied in the shade of the river, mayhap shedding her shoes and stockings to dangle her feet in the cool, green water. She discarded the thought immediately. Catherine wouldn't delay on such an important errand. Not when so many bruised and aching combatants needed tending to.

A dozen, less sanguine explanations for the girl's delay in returning to the keep raced through her mind as she hurried after Hugh. Wolves and long-tusked boars roamed the nearby woods. Poachers, who could turn desperate if caught. Bands of robbers that might have been attracted by the tournament's jongleurs, fortune tellers and merry makers' purses jingling with coins. And, before Eleanor could banish the bleak thought, came the dread that the girl had mayhap sought a drastic solution to her dread of the marriage bed.

Worry sat like a stone on her shoulders as William Marshal and Sir Giles rushed out of the keep in answer to Hugh's summons. Several of the other knights who'd participated in the tourney joined the crowd that quickly gathered, Eleanor saw, FitzGilbert among them. After a few quick words with Hugh, they too, joined the search. Stable hands saddled fresh mounts while squires rushed to retrieve the armor and weapons they'd been cleaning. A detachment of men-at-arm made themselves ready, as well.

With no orders to the contrary, the grooms had saddled one of Hugh's hunters. He chose not to wait for Sirocco to be brought out instead. Mounting, he issued swift instructions.

"Giles, we'll make for the river. You follow it north. I'll go south. If you will search the woods behind the keep, Sir William, FitzGilbert can scour those near the tourney grounds. I misdoubt Catherine would go that far afoot, but we'd best cover all possibilities."

Wheeling, Hugh swung toward the barbican.

Guy came running from the kennels. Jasmine raced as close as a shadow behind him. "Wait, Hugh! I'll help look."

He pushed through the crowd too late. Hugh had already cleared the gate and the others followed at a fast trot. Thoroughly disgusted, Guy kicked at a nearby pile of muck.

"Sard it!"

His disgust vanished instantly when he turned and met his mother's outraged glance. Like an avenging Viking princess, Lady Alice surged forward and snared her youngest's ear in a punishing grip.

"I disbelieve what I just heard come from your lips! Father Anselm will have you on your knees the rest of this day and night. *After* I administer the thrashing you deserve."

"Ow! Ow! Ow!"

Guy hopped and flapped his arms as she yanked him across the bailey. Eleanor had heard her father mutter the same vile oath when he was too far gone in his cups to censor his tongue, so she wasn't as shocked by it as Lady Alice. And, in truth, she suspected poor Guy was bearing the brunt of his mother's wrath over what she'd interrupted in the garden.

Eleanor would have to face that wrath, too. But not, she decided, until Catherine was found. And the matter of marriage was settled between herself and FitzGilbert. She would stay well out of Lady Alice's way until then. She, and Jasmine both.

That was certainly her intent. But the hours dragged by, one after another, and no word came from any of the searchers. Tension mounted until Eleanor could no longer pretend to stitch an altar cloth or keep Jasmine confined with her in the ladies' bower. Once released, her sister raced for the stairs to see if she could determine the fate of her boon companion.

"Don't disturb Guy at his penance!"

Eleanor had not the least certainty that her command would be obeyed. Jasmine's loyalties, once fixed, ran deep and true. The older sister only prayed that the younger would not tempt the boy to steal horses from the stables and mount their own search for the missing Catherine.

Eleanor descended the stairs more slowly and sought out Lady Alice. She could not beg forgiveness for that kiss. Nor for the heat that had flashed through her like a raging tide the night before the tourney. But she *could* swear yet again that Hugh had not dishonored her or himself. Except, she amended with an inner sigh, in their thoughts.

She found Lady Alice in the great hall. Lady Margaret crowded close behind her, as did Father Anselem and the lieutenant Hugh had ordered to take charge of guarding the keep. Kneeling before them was a man-at-arms who'd obviously ridden hard and fast. Sweat flattened his coarse hair to his skull and so much mud covered his surcoat that it almost obscured the device on its front.

As muddied as it was, Eleanor recognized the black wolf's head immediately. He was Penhammond's man. Sent to deliver what looked like a crumpled note to Lady Alice.

"He's found Catherine!" Eleanor exclaimed, hurrying across the hall. "Please say Penhammond's found her!"

Lady Alice raised her eyes from the note. Her face was a mottled white, her reply a raw whisper. "Aye, he's found her."

"She's not…? She's not dead?"

"No."

"Injured? Dear God, is she hurt?"

"No."

"Then what?" Relieved and confused at the same time, Eleanor gestured to the parchment. "What says he?"

"He says…" Lady Alice stopped, swallowed, and began again in a voice that rapidly gathered both fire and fury. "He says he's in need of a rich wife. He'll take Catherine, or he'll take you…as long as you bring him the rubies that constitute your dower. But he'll have one or the other of you in his bed this night."

Chapter Eleven

"Where is he?"

Fury and fear for timid Cathrine hammered at Eleanor as she rounded on the man-at-arms who'd delivered the missive. Obviously unaware of its contents until Lady Alice had read it aloud, the courier had turned as pale as the underbelly of a carp. Still on one knee, he began to shake so violently he almost toppled over.

"I… I…."

"Where's your master?"

The courier was still trying to stammer out a reply when the Hugh's lieutenant swung a vicious backhand and knocked the man into the rushes.

"He'll answer soon enough when we put him on the rack. You!" he shouted to two underlings. "Drag this vermin down to…."

"Hold!" Eleanor commanded. "Let him speak. Come, man. Tell us! Where did you leave the baron?"

Blood spurted from the messenger's nose. Fear oozed from every other orifice. "At the… At the crossroads to Chester, lady. He said he would leave a troop there to escort you further."

"He was so sure I would come, then?"

"I…I don't know, lady. Just that I was to deliver the message and bring you to the crossroads."

"We must get word to Hugh at once," Lady Alice interjected. "And to Sir Giles and the others. Father Anselem, will you pen the notes?"

"Of course."

As the priest hurried off in search of pen and parchment, Lady Alice directed the lieutenant to have horses saddled.

"Include Sirocco among them," Eleanor command.

The lieutenant stopped, swung back. "Why, lady? Sir Hugh has said that only he is to ride the beast."

"Oh, so? Do you forget who delivered him to Sir Hugh?"

"No, but…"

"Eleanor!" Lady Alice spun around. "You cannot mean to go to Penhammond!"

"I do."

"That's beyond foolish! Hugh will go to this crossroads. Or William Marshal or Ian FitzGilbert, if they return first."

"We daren't wait! We don't know how far the men have gone in search of Catherine, but we do know none of them planned to scour the road to Chester. By the time we send word to turn in that direction, it'll be dark. And…" Her gaze locked with Lady Alice's. "Penhammond may well make good his threat. If he takes a bride to his bed this night," she finished grimly, "I would far rather it be me than Catherine."

The look that passed between them acknowledged the brutal fact that Eleanor could endure a quick wedding and rough bedding with more fortitude than Catherine. Or mayhap use skill and cunning to avoid both.

"With luck and a flagon or two of wine," she said softly, "I may be able to hold him off until Hugh arrives."

Lady Alice's grip tightened until it near crushed Eleanor's bones before she reluctantly agreed. "You must."

"I'll do my best. In the meantime, do you have the keys to the storeroom?"

"The storeroom? Yes, of course."

"I need you to open it for me."

"Now? Why?"

"I must retrieve the rubies. If matters don't go as we hope and I'm forced to marry the man, those accursed stones may make our union a little more palatable."

"Oh, Eleanor!"

"There's no time for further argumentation. Please, take me to the counting room. And you, Lady Margaret, would you be so kind as to find a traveling basket for me? One large enough to hold some clean linens and another gown, in case I should have need of it."

"Of course." Sir Gile's wife picked up skirts, took two steps, and swung back. "What of Jasmine?"

"Oh, Lud!"

How could Eleanor have forgotten her sister? Jittering and jolting like summer lightning, her mind jumped from one alternative to another for dealing with the headstrong, unpredictable girl in this crisis. Desperate, she turned to the lieutenant. "When last I saw my sister, she was with Guy. Would you send someone to find her, and have her meet me in the ladies' bower?"

He nodded, then aimed a kick at Penhammond's still cowering courier. "Get up, lout, and cease your sniveling. You'll live for a few hours more. Until we find your master, at least."

Once in the storeroom, Eleanor hurriedly pulled out the key that always dangled between her breasts. Despite the worry scoring deep grooves in Lady Alice's forehead, her eyes went as round as trebuchet stones when she unlocked her casket.

"By all the saints!" Jaw slack, Hugh's mother gaped at the glittering jewels. "This is in truth a king's ransom."

Eleanor scooped up the loose stones that had escaped their pouch and dropped them back in the drawstring bag. That done, she hurriedly sorted through the remaining contents.

"The emerald ring, the pearls and sapphires, the gold collar… Those are for Jasmine and my daughters, should I have any. Will you keep them safe until either she or I can claim them?"

Still dumbstruck, Lady Alice dragged her gaze from the treasure trove and nodded.

"Thank you." Eleanor hesitated a few precious seconds. "And I beg you, please don't think too harshly of what you saw in the garden. I know the lust your son stirs in me - and I in him - is a sin. But I swear Hugh has not allowed that lust to bend his honor."

"Would that he *had*!"

The exclamation burst from the older woman with much the same force as the vile oath that had landed Guy in such trouble. Eleanor blinked, sure she'd not heard right.

Lady Alice saw her reaction and screwed her face into a grimace. "I'm not a fool, child. Nor is Catherine. We can both see that Hugh desires you with a hunger that makes our hearts ache for both of you."

"We will not yield to that hunger. We *won't*."

"I know." Lady Alice's gaze dropped to the silken pouch. When it lifted again, her faded blue eyes were as bleak as a winter sea. "The more I think on it, the more I wonder if you'll find that Catherine will not allow herself to be traded for your precious rubies."

"She cannot give herself to Penhammond! He may not use her as harshly as her father did *his* wives but he won't use her gently, either. Holy Virgin! I must get to them."

Whirling, Eleanor rushed out of the counting room and up the winding tower stairs. She sped past the great hall, continued past the landing for the lord's chamber, and burst into the ladies' bower. The first sight that greeted her was her sister with feet spread wide, the hem of her robe coated with mud, and one fist wrapped around the hilt of her precious dagger.

"Jasmine! Thank goodness they found you."

"I was at the fish pond," she said with a mutinous glance at Lady Alice. "Skipping stones until Guy finishes his penance."

"Yes, well, something's come up and…"

"Lady Margaret told me. She says we go to the baron who has the face of a ferret."

"Not *we*, pet. I go. You will wait here until I return or…or send for you."

"No!" The hand wrapped around the hilt of the dagger went white at the knuckles. "He's a pig, that one. Does he lay one hand on you, I'll pierce his nose and put a ring in it. Or I'll slice off his bollocks. He can join the ranks of eunuchs and…"

"Oh, Jasmine."

Desperate to get to Catherine, Eleanor dropped the silk purse atop the basket Lady Margaret had found for her and sank to one knee before her sister.

"I don't have time to argue with you. Promise you'll stay with Lady Alice until I return or send for you."

"But…"

"There's no time for buts, my sweet. Promise me. *Please!*"

A sulky nod was all she got, but it was enough. Jasmine was as quick as a fox and like as not to slip away from any task she had no taste for. But her word once given was as solid as…

As Hugh's, Eleanor thought, near choking on the irony.

She pulled her sister close for a quick kiss, then hurried to the chest holding her things. She would take only what she could cram in the basket but must needs plan for the worst. With Lady Margaret hovering at her shoulder, she rummaged through the contents.

"I'll take this gown. And these veils. And a night robe."

While the two of them hurriedly folded the stack of garments, Lady Alice unlocked an upright chest with one of the keys dangling from her chatelaine's belt and bent over the contents. When she found what she wanted, she beckoned to Eleanor.

"You will not know of such things," she said in a low, urgent whisper, "but there are ways to lessen the pain of a breaching."

Eleanor hesitated, loathe to tell her that women spoke of such matters freely in a land where men took multiple wives and concubines. Still, her eyes widened at the blunt advice the older woman offered. Then Lady Alice pressed a small square of linen into her hand.

"This contains a mix of powdered pomegranate, juniper and rue. If you *are* forced to bed with Penhammond, as soon as you are able dampen the cloth and insert it where he thrust into you."

When Eleanor lifted a questioning gaze, Lady Alice's mouth tipped into a tight smile. "The priests say it is a sin to pray that a husband's seed won't quicken in our wombs. Even the seed of a husband who might take us by force. If priests were the ones giving birth, however, I suspect they would soon sing a different psalm."

"I suspect so, too," Eleanor agreed with a strangled laugh. "Now I must go."

When she went to add the linen square to the basket, however, she saw no sight of the drawstring bag containing the rubies. Whirling, she faced Lady Margaret.

"The silk pouch? Did you pack it inside?"

"No, I…"

"I have it." Jasmine raised an arm. The bag dangled by its strings from her fingers. "I said an incantation over it," she informed Eleanor defiantly. "If the baron hurts you, scorpions will crawl out of his nose and boils the size of camel turds will raise on his arse."

"Oh, sweet Lord! Let's hope I don't see either."

Bending, she swept her sister into a fierce hug. Then she stuffed the pouch into the basket and hurried down the winding stone staircase.

When she gained the bailey, the lieutenant of the guard confirmed there was still no sign of or word from the search parties. He also insisted that he and his troop would personally escort the Lady Eleanor to her rendezvous with Baron Penhammond.

The man who'd delivered the baron's message slumped in his saddle. One eye was puffed and swollen shut. Dried blood traced from his nose to his chin. Bruises colored both cheeks. Eleanor might have spared him a moment's pity if the magnificent destrier being led into the cobbled yard hadn't claimed her instant attention.

She asked one of the lieutenant's men to affix her basket to the saddle while she ran a gentle hand over Sirocco's milky neck.

"Aye, my beauty," she crooned before using the mounting block to gain the saddle. "Let's away."

To the intense relief of both Eleanor and the courier still nursing his bruises, the promised escort was waiting at the stone that marked the road to Chester. For a tense moment, however, it looked as though they and Eleanor's escorts might come to blows. Pikes lowered. Swords whipped out. Terse inquiries led to an exchange of insults. Only after Eleanor insisted the baron's men take her at once to their master did a wary truce take hold.

"Where do we go?" she asked as the small troop wheeled into position.

"The abbey of Saint Swithin's, lady."

At her insistence, they rode hard and rode fast. The summer sun sank lower with each mile. Fighting a sick fear for Catherine, Eleanor prayed they would not be too late. So she almost sobbed with relief when they turned off the main road and followed a dirt track to an abbey that dominated a stretch of plowed fields and flowering orchards.

Like so many great monasteries and nunneries, this one reflected the wealth accumulated by those in holy orders. The church itself was solid and square in the Roman style, but the refectory where the residents ate and worked boasted a high, arched roof and windows of leaded glass that blazed in the last rays of the setting sun. A colonnade of sculpted pillars connected the church and refectory. Another colonnade led to the kitchens, storerooms, and a long, low building Eleanor guessed was the dormitory. Some distance from the cloister were a scattering outbuildings that attested to the abbey's wealth and self-sufficiency. She spotted a mill, a bakehouse, stables, cattle stalls as her troop approached.

Priories and abbeys such as this were by far the best places to seek refuge while traveling. Monks and nuns were bound by holy vows to provide food and shelter, while the sanctity of the church assured the safety of those within. Peasants would stretch out on straw pallets in the dormitories, the men separated from women, of course. Merchants and others claiming goodman's status might gain a private alcove. Titled guests would most likely be accorded a private chamber with furnishings and comforts in keeping with the size of the gift they offered in recompense for their lodgings.

An abbey as rich as this would be home to a dozen or more monks. Eleanor had heard that her namesake, Queen Eleanor, had founded an even more magnificent abbey in her native province of Aquitaine. One where both brothers and sisters lived in harmony and were governed by an abbess. Most such establishments, however, were governed by an ordained priest who might be convinced to perform a marriage without the pesky necessity of gaining approval from a bishop.

Eleanor dismounted, stretching to work the kinks from her back, and felt her heart beat hard against her ribs when a tonsured brother in a black robe answered the pull of the bell.

"Welcome to St Swithin's," he murmured, his voice low and his eyes downcast. "Are you the Lady Eleanor?"

"I am."

"Your men may take the horses to the stables. You may come with me."

Exmoor's lieutenant pushed forward. "I go with my lady."

"You cannot." Voice still low, eyes still pinned to the dirt, he shook his head. "My orders are to admit only her."

Her faithful guardian gripped the hilt of his sword. "Then you'll get other orders, man, or I'll…"

Eleanor stilled him with a quick hand on his leather gauntlet. "I'll summon you if I need you."

"Sir Hugh will skin me alive if I leave you unprotected, lady!"

"Not if I tell him it was by my orders."

He set his jaw, unconvinced.

"I swear I'll summon you if I need you," Eleanor said, anxiety for Catherine adding steel to her voice. "Please, unhook my basket and hand it to me. Don't stable the horses, however. I'll try to convince the baron to release Lady Catherine and allow me to take her back to Exmoor. If I fail, I'll remain here in her stead, but you must get her away from Saint Swithin's as quickly as possible."

It was just as she'd guessed. Penhammond's rank had secured him a chamber that contained a table of polished oak, two carved chairs set on either side of a fireplace, an illuminated Bible on a stand of twisted iron, and a bed with heavy curtains to keep out drafts. Eleanor gained only a fleeting impression of the furnishings, however, as her entrance brought one of the room's two occupants springing from her chair.

"You came! Oh, Eleanor, you came!"

Bursting into sobs, Catherine rushed across the room. Eleanor dropped her basket and folded the girl in a fierce embrace.

"Of course, I came. You must have known I would." She aimed a glance as deadly as a poisoned arrow at the man sprawled in the other chair. "Did you think I would leave you to deal with such a plague-ridden white-liver by yourself?"

"White-liver?" Penhammond echoed, his lips curling. "I've been called many things, but never a coward."

"How else would you describe a poltroon who abducts a helpless maid?"

"You're misinformed, lady. I merely rescued a maid who'd wandered away from her escort and became lost." His sneer tipped into something close to a smile. "And I must confess Lady Catherine is hardly helpless. Her claws are sharp."

When he angled his chin enough to display the four livid scratches that scored his right cheek, Eleanor hugged the girl even tighter.

"Good for you!"

Catherine raised her head at that. "Would that I had clawed out his eyes!"

"He'll lose them and more when Hugh comes," Eleanor promised fiercely.

If he came in time.

If he did not…

"And why is Exmoor not with you?" Penhammond asked, as if reading her mind. "He can't defile the sanctity of an abbey by mounting an armed attack, of course, but I expected him to at least show his face."

"He'll come," Eleanor promised savagely. "You should not think to leave this abbey unchallenged."

"I don't." Penhammond's teeth gleamed under the silky black of his mustache. "Which is why I've sent for a full detachment of my men. They should arrive at any moment. And why we should get this bothersome business of a marriage out of the way quickly."

"You cannot force either of us to wed you."

"Oh, but I can. I've already arranged the matter with the abbot. As it turns out, he's much afeared of losing his fat sinecure when Richard arrives in England. It seems the good abbot threatened to excommunicate our princeling for rebelling against his father, the anointed King Henry. And worse, he refuses to open St Swithin's treasure chests to pay Richard's Saladin tax. Evidently he feels the monies collected by the church belong only to the church. So in exchange for my oath to take up arms to keep him in office, he'll marry me to any wife of my choosing."

He strolled forward, his dark eyes glinting. Hastily, Eleanor thrust Catherine behind her and met his sardonic smile with a look of pure ice.

"Then you'd best choose me, Penhammond, for Exmoor and Catherine have exchanged sacred vows. Wed her in defiance of those vows and you risk excommunication."

Such a threat would daunt most men. Women, too. They shied away from the very thought of being denied the sacraments and condemning themselves to everlasting Hell. The sly look on his face told Eleanor she'd played right into his hands, however.

"So be it. I choose you, lady. Assuming, of course, you've brought your dower."

The avenues of escape were closing fast. Eleanor had only one last card to play. "I have. I will give them to you and go to your bed without a fight…with one condition."

"You will go to my bed regardless."

"Then you'd best not fall sleep, this night or any other!"

"*Jesu*, what a firebrand you are." Desire sparked in his eyes and added a husky note to his voice. "All right, lady, speak your condition."

"Release Catherine now, this moment, and send her back to Exmoor. My escort waits outside. Once she's ahorse and safely on her way, we'll conclude this farce."

"Do I have your word on that?"

Her brows lifted. "You would trust the word of a mere female?"

"I would trust yours."

That surprised her. For a traitorous moment she wondered if marriage to the baron might not be so dire. He was still strong and virile enough to father children. And bold enough to snatch at fate.

"You have my word."

With a triumphant nod, he strode to the door and summoned another tonsured brother. "Escort the Lady Catherine to the gates and give her into the hands of the troop wearing the eagle of Exmoor."

Her sobs abated, Catherine thrust out from behind Eleanor's protective back. "I will not leave you with this monster."

"Get you gone, Cat. The baron and I will deal together as we must."

"No!" Her voice quavering with false bravado, Catherine stood her ground. "Take me to wife, Penhammond. I will make you a far more docile mate than Eleanor."

"I doubt that not," he drawled. "But it seems I've developed a taste for a certain flame-haired wench."

"Go, Catherine," Eleanor ordered, her nerves raw from playing this cat-and-mouse game. "Go now."

"No, I…"

"Go! Do your duty as a wife, and I will do mine."

The fierce command jerked Catherine's head back. The look in her eyes was so much like that of an arrow-shot doe that Eleanor had to ball her fists to keep from reaching for her. She could only watch with an ache in her heart while Hugh's betrothed gave a small nod and left the chamber without another word.

Chapter Twelve

As the echo of Catherine's footsteps faded, stillness crept through the chamber. Eleanor could almost hear her heart kicking against her chest. She stood unmoving until the flame in one of the fat candles illuminating the chamber hit a grease pocket. Hissing and spitting, its shadow danced like a drunken archer on the wall.

Penhammond made a half-hearted effort to cut through the tension that swirled as thick as winter fog. With a laconic wave, he gestured to the carved chairs. "You've had a hard ride, lady. Take your ease."

Eleanor gave a cool nod and accepted the invitation. She and her escort had, in truth, traveled hard and fast. Fear for Catherine had sat heavy on her shoulders the entire way and added its weight to the wave of fatigue that suddenly washed through her.

"The abbot awaits my summons," Penhammond said, those dark eyes fixed on her face, "but I will not have you fainting as you say your vows."

"I do not faint."

She took great pride in the fact that her reply contained the perfect mix of condescension and icy disdain. Penhammond accepted both with a half bow.

"I'll be sure to remember that. Nevertheless, will you at least take some wine before we get this done?"

Eleanor would rather drink boiled birch bark than take anything from this man's hand. But dust from the ride clogged her throat, and wine would help fortify her for what was to come.

"I will."

Her nod was as regal as her tone, but when she reached for the goblet he held out to her she couldn't keep her hand from trembling. The baron didn't fail to note it, damn his soul, and waited only until she'd fortified herself with a long swallow to cut to the matter as yet unspoken between them.

"Before I take you to the abbot, lady, I would see your dower."

It was no more than she'd expected. No more than what she'd intended when she'd decided to leave Outremer to seek husbands for herself and Jasmine here, in the land of their father. Yet her courage almost failed her as she set aside the wine goblet and retrieved her traveling basket. Once she handed over the rubies, she would have sold herself to this man.

As well him as any other, she thought with an ache in her heart. The man she hungered for, the one she would have given herself to so eagerly, was pledged to Catherine.

Her back stiffened. Her chin lifted. She'd chosen her fate. Best to be done with it. Mouth set, she fished the silken pouch from the basket and tossed it to the baron.

"I think you'll find this more than sufficient to your needs."

"We must hope so, lady." With a saturnine smile, he worked the strings of the pouch. "Sadly, my needs have grown ever more pressing. And when Richard claims his crown, as he soon will, I fear he'll…"

He broke off, his breath hissing, as he tipped some of the contents of the pouch into his palm. For a few seconds Eleanor thought it must have been the fire of the rubies that stopped his breath. Then his fist closed, his gaze lifted to hers, and the fury in his face almost sent her back a pace.

"You dare to play me false?" he said softly, dangerously.

"False?"

He stalked toward her, as swift and deadly as a serpent. This time she did back away. Two quick, stumbling steps that brought her up against the table. It blocked further retreat, while Penhammond loomed taut and menacing before her.

"You think I'll not take you?" he said, the fury still darkening his face. "That I'll not make you pay a forfeit for this game you play?"

"*What* game?"

In answer, he raised his fist. Eleanor thought at first he meant to strike her. She braced herself but would not cringe before him. Then he opened his fist, and her stunned gaze fixed on the dull gray pebbles in his palm.

"What…? Where…?" Enlightenment hit like a bolt shot from a crossbow. "Oh, Sweet Mary!"

She couldn't help herself. Laughter rose up on a swift, unstoppable tide. It burst out, echoed through the chamber, and bounced off the walls. Penhammond's look of blank surprise only added to her mirth.

"Jasmine," she choked out when she could speak at all.

"That changling you call sister?"

She nodded, gasping for breath. "She was…skipping stones…at the duck pond."

Penhammond took a moment to untangle the explanation. "Your sister has the rubies?"

"I would…wager so."

With a vicious curse, he whipped out his arm. The pebbles flew across the chamber and rained against the wall before plinking down among the rushes.

"You'll do more than wager, lady. We'll ride back to Exmoor to retrieve your dower. Before we do, however, you'll pay and pay well for this…"

"Oh, for the love of all the saints! Cease your threats!" Swallowing the last of her mirth, Eleanor put a hand to his shoulder and gave it a shove. "Move away, if you please. I'm done cowering against this table."

Once again she'd surprised him. The violence he'd come so close to unleashing receded from both his face and his stance. In its place came a grudging respect.

"You don't frighten easily, do you?"

"Not easily, although you did make my heart skip for a moment or two. But we'll deal much better with each other if we refrain from such unnecessary commotions in the future."

He cocked his head. "So we're to have a future?"

"Only if we wed. You won't get anything from me except a knife blade at your throat if you use me as a whore."

His mouth tipped. "I begin to wonder if even a purse full of rubies is sufficient dower for a woman with as strong a will as you appear to possess."

"My father would have told you it is not," she replied tartly. "But the the choice is yours, baron."

"So it is. Come, then, and we'll set the abbot to work."

His words confirmed her fate. As he escorted her to the door, Eleanor felt as though her chest was encased in ice. Once in the vast, echoing hall, he signaled to the men lounging against one of the pillars supporting the arched colonnade. They'd surrendered their weapons, as required by all who sought sanctuary in a house of God, but the snarling wolf embroidered on their surcoats left no doubt who they owed fealty to.

One was young, a boy hardly bearded. But his eyes were as cold and hard as his lord's. Penhammond's squire, Eleanor guessed. Or mayhap his son? The other was battle scarred and sent her a swift glance of what looked like pity before Penhammond issued a terse command.

"With me."

The abbey church boasted a long nave cut by a transept that faded into darkness at either end. Candles smoked and flickered at sparse intervals along the aisle. The scent of incense hung on the dank air. Shadowed side altars showed only the faint glimmer of wood panels painted with images of the dying Christ, the ascending Mary, and various tortured saints.

The monks were at compline, their last service before they retired for the night. They chanted in Latin, and the quiet harmony of their voices seemed to give peace to the handful of pilgrims who stood at a respectful distance behind them. Penhammond, Eleanor and the two men-at-arms took their place among the pilgrims and waited for the service to be done.

"Are you ready?" Penhammond asked when the chants ended.

She lifted her chin. "Yes."

The monks filed out, their tonsured heads pale in the dim light. More than one cast a curious glance at the richly clothed couple who'd waited for the service to end. Penhammond ignored their curiosity and wrapped a proprietary hand around Eleanor's arm and drew her toward the chancel. Like the side chapels, the main altar was framed by paintings on wood. But these stretched across a series of six tall panels and were etched in gold and silver and studded with gems that gleamed even in the dim light. Below the center panel was a solid gold reliquary that Eleanor guessed contained the bones or fingers or some other body part of Saint Swithin.

The abbot hurried forward to meet them. Given the size of his abbey, Eleanor had expected a plump, lavishly robed priest. Whatever riches this man coveted for his order obviously didn't extend to his own comfort, however. He was so thin that Eleanor suspected he fasted more than he did not. And far from being richly robed, he wore a habit as black and plain as those of his monks.

His eyes shone with a fervor that raised the hair on the back of her neck, however, and the first words out of his mouth belied his humble appearance. "Have you secured her dower? And the portion you've pledged to the abbey?"

Penhammond dodged the question with a skill Eleanor could only admire. "I have the lady to hand, do I not?"

"Yes, yes. Let's get on with it, then. Kneel."

Eleanor sank to her knees, her heart leaden in her chest. Penhammond took his place beside her. The abbot leafed through his psalter to find the right passage and lifted his hand to make the sign of the cross over them.

"*In nomine patris et filii et...*"

He broke off, frowning as the tramp of shod feet on stone carried clearly from the rear of the dimly lit church.

"Hold!"

The command echoed down the tall, arched nave. Penhammond twisted violently around, Eleanor gasped a quick prayer of thanksgiving, and the abbot voiced venomous outrage. "Who dares profane God's sanctuary?"

On a wave of whispers and startled exclamations, the pilgrims parted to make way as a figure swathed in a heavy riding cloak came down the aisle.

Not Exmoor, Eleanor saw as fierce disappointment quickly tempered with relief ripped through her. Spilling blood here, on holy ground, would damn him beyond all hope of redemption.

And yet....

And yet...

There he was there! Following hard on the heels of the other. Even in the dim light, she couldn't mistake his broad shoulders and the eagle on his surcoat. She surged to her feet, her eyes so fixed on him and the men who crowded through the entry behind him that it took her several more seconds to realize the person they followed down the dimly lit aisle was female.

Not Catherine. Not Lady Alice. No one Eleanor could identify until Penhammond muttered a short, savage oath. He tempered his tone and called out in a voice that carried both steel and ice.

"You honor us by standing as witness to our marriage, my lady Queen."

The queen?

Here?

Stunned, Eleanor recalled snippets of conversation from the past few days. The Saladin tithe. The queen going on progress to make sure it went into the royal coffers. The possibility she might attend the tournament at Exmoor.

Still shocked, she could only gape as the queen shoved back the hood of her riding cloak. Eleanor had grown up hearing so many tales of this woman. Her bravery. Her boldness. Her legendary beauty that was still sung of by troubadours and poets.

All three showed in the face illuminated by the flickering candles. Despite the sixteen years of bleak confinement she'd emerged from mere weeks ago, the queen wore her sixty-seven years with haughty grace. Only when she stopped a few feet away did those candles reveal the network of lines webbing the corners of her eyes and a sagging chin her wimple couldn't quite disguise.

Her voice held not a single quaver of age, however, as she address Penhammond. "You mistake the matter, Baron. I have not come to witness a marriage."

"This lady is sworn to me. We will wed this night."

A violent movement wrenched Eleanor's stunned gaze to Hugh, now pushing forward. "Not this night, Penhammond," he snarled, "nor any other."

The queen whipped out an arm to stop him before he'd taken more than a step. Her haughty gaze returned to the baron. "You have proof that she is sworn to you? A marriage contract, with her dower rights laid out and properly attested to?"

Eleanor felt Penhammond stiffen beside her. "There's been no time to draw up contracts. But we have given pledges to each other."

The queen's mouth twisted in a smile that held no trace of mirth. "And we all know, do we not, the weight such pledges hold in the eyes of man *and* God."

Her voice rose, sharpened. "Abbot, I require a chamber for the night for myself and my ladies. Housing for my men, and those of Sir Hugh. *Now*," she added impatiently.

The abbot knew, as did all others present, that his future and that of his rich abbey hung on whether the queen's son could hold the crown he was enroute to claim. That issue was most certainly in doubt. At this moment, however, his wisest course was to accede to her command. He snapped his psalter shut and assumed an unctuous expression that fooled no one.

"Saint Swithin's is most honored to offer you and your party shelter, lady queen. I will show you to a chamber."

She nodded and crooked an imperious finger at Eleanor. "You, girl. Come with me."

Eleanor abandoned her would-be groom at the altar without a word and followed the queen. And as she approached Hugh, she only had time for a quick plea with him for understanding.

"I had to come."

The swift, icy anger in his reply was all the more potent for being so tightly leashed. "No, you did not."

"Hugh..."

"Get you to the queen. We'll speak later."

Later, it turned out, was late indeed. First the ladies accompanying the queen had to see to her comfort. They fluttered about the chamber allotted to them in what Eleanor soon recognized was a well-rehearsed ritual. Small wonder they knew just what they were about, having accompanied their royal mistress on progress for several weeks now.

Servants were sent for bread, fruits, meats and honeyed wine. Dusty cloaks were whisked away. Traveling chests were unpacked. The bed was remade with fine linens. The queen was relieved of her boots, bliaut and headdress, then eased into slippers and a richly embroidered bed robe belted with a twisted gold cord. Without the wimple, her hair showed more white than red and the lines in her face etched deeper.

Only then did the queen sink into an armchair by the fire and point to the stool next to her. "Sit here, girl, and tell me about your years in Outremer. And how you came to possess what rumors say is a king's ransom in jewels."

Once again, Eleanor recounted her exploits since her father's death. Mention of the sultan of J'bara brought startled exclamation.

"J'bara! I remember him! Fat and as long-nosed as a camel... Unless..." Her forehead creased. "I may be thinking of his father. Or grandfather," she amended, the frown deepening.

"If you are," Eleanor assured her, "the family resemblance runs true."

"And J'bara wanted you for his harem?"

"He did. And sent many lavish gifts to tempt me. If I'd not had to search for my father once in just such a place, I might indeed have been swayed."

"Your father would dare to enter a harem?"

"He would," Eleanor confirmed with a laugh that was as fond as it was exasperated. "I loved him dearly, but I would be the first to admit that upon occasion he imbibed too freely and - ah - acted with imprudence. That wasn't my only visit to a harem, though. I spent some hours with the sultan's wives. They were so exotic and richly bejeweled. But bored beyond measure with their restricted lives and all as plump as partridges from the sweetmeats and pickled eggs they consumed by the dishful."

"So instead of becoming one of J'Bara's wives or concubines, you decided to sail for a home you'd never seen."

"I did."

"You were brave to make such a journey on your own."

"I'll admit to more than one attack of nerves during the long voyage," Eleanor confessed ruefully. "Pirates gave chase to our ship twice, but we managed to make safe harbor each time."

"Ahhhh, girl, such an adventurous life you've lived in your short years."

"No more adventurous than yours, majesty."

A far away look crept into the queen's eyes, and distant memories brought a smile to her lips. "No more than mine," she agreed softly.

If only a third of all the tales Eleanor had heard of this formidable woman were true, she cast every queen and duchess in Christendom into the shade. She sat silent while the queen savored her memories for several long moments before giving her shoulders a little shake.

"Enough of the past, child. Tell me truthfully. Do you want Penhammond for husband?"

"Truthfully? I do not. But I came to England in search of a husband and...." She forced a shrug. "He will do as well as any, I suppose. Once I've brought him to heel, that is."

The queen's brows rose. "You think you can?"

"Most assuredly. My father always swore I would drive the devil himself to drink. I suspect Penhammond would agree ere long."

"I begin to suspect he would," the queen said with a glimmer of laughter in her eyes. "But what of Exmoor? From what I gleaned when we met on the road, he's not best pleased with this match."

Eleanor keep her smile firmly in place. "He's not. But much as he thinks to exercise a kinsman's rights over me, he has promised to give me final say in who I take to my bed."

"Exmoor?" The queen's brows soared. "*Exmoor* made such a promise?"

"Not without some argumentation, I admit. But I…"

"Yes, yes, I know. You would drive the devil himself to drink."

The sat in silence for some moments before the queen broke it with a sigh. "We can do better for you than Penhammond, girl. I will think on it, and discuss it with my son once he arrives. Betimes, I will take you into my keeping. Go now, speak with Exmoor, as he near rode us all into the ground in his determination to get to you. Then return, and claim a place among my ladies."

"I have a sister, lady queen. She's but six years old. If I am to go with you, I beg you will allow her to come as well."

"Of course. One small girl will be no burden to my household."

Wisely, Eleanor held her tongue.

"We'll send for her to join us on the road. Now go, speak with Exmoor while I take my weary bones to bed."

One of her ladies sent a lackey to summon a lay brother. The man expressed shock at being told to escort a lady to the Lord of Exmoor. "I cannot. Women are not allowed in the men's dormitories."

"Then take me to where I may wait for him," Eleanor instructed impatiently, "and bring him there."

Still doubtful, the brother led her through a series of dank corridors lit at distant intervals only by the moonlight showing through narrow window slits. His rope-soled sandals bounced echoes off the square cut floor stones and the candle he carried sputtered in the drafts. After a series of twists and turns that warned Eleanor she would have a time of it finding her way back to the queen's chamber, he paused beside an unadorned wooden door.

"If you will wait within, lady, I will fetch the lord of Exmoor."

He drew another candle from the pocket of his robe, lit it with the one he carried and passed it to Eleanor before disappearing into the shadows. She had to dip her head to enter what looked to her very much like a penitent's cell. Little more than six eight or ten feet in length and width, it contained only a straw pallet, a chamberpot, and a crucifix. In the flickering candlelight, Eleanor spied a niche in the stone wall. She tilted her candle, dripped a puddle of soft wax, then fixed the stump so it would stand. That done, she had nothing to do but try to compose a calm, rational explanation of why she did not, *could* not wait for Hugh's return before riding to Catherine's rescue.

Surely he would see that she'd had no choice. That she'd had no way of knowing how long it would take for word of Catherine's whereabouts to reach him. That she couldn't have let Penhammond terrorize the girl into a quick wedding and bedding.

Although in truth Catherine's brave attempt to offer herself up on the altar of the baron's lust had surprised both Penhammond and Eleanor. She would tell Exmoor of that noble attempt, she decided. Let him see that his betrothed had more spine to her than even she herself realized.

She'd tell him also of the queen's decision to take her and Jasmine into keeping. Pray God that would douse, or at least diminish, the burning need Exmoor no doubt now harbored to gut Penhammond and hang his entrails from the nearest tree.

When she heard the thud of footsteps in the hall, she composed her face and marshaled her thoughts. Then the door opened, and Exmoor ducked under the low lintel. He'd laid off his surcoat and mail and wore only a loose-sleeved linen shirt and his leather chausses, buckled by a wide belt.

And before Eleanor could get out so much as a greeting, he kicked the wood panel shut, crossed the tiny cell in two furious strides and had her up against the wall.

"You little fool!"

Since she was neither particularly little nor a fool, she started to protest. He cut her off by bringing his mouth down on hers with bruising force.

Chapter Thirteen

The kiss was savage, laced with fire and fury that burned through every thought, every caution, every restraint Eleanor had struggled for so long to place on her emotions.

The need to answer his kiss jolted through her. Fast. Searing. So violent she clawed her arms free from where they'd been pinned against the wall and flung them around Hugh's neck.

This hour, she thought wildly as she pressed her mouth even more fiercely against his. This night. If nothing else, they'd have this stolen time together. She refused to let herself think of the penance this wanton conduct would earn her. Done in an abbey, no less! She was beyond caring for anything but the press of Exmoor's body against hers and the fierce need it roused in her.

Their mouths were still locked when Hugh wrapped a hard arm around her waist. He broke the kiss only long enough to drag her the few feet to the straw pallet.

"Say nothing," he snarled as he released her. Unbuckling his belt, he let it drop before he took her down to the straw. "Not one word. I'm still of a mind to beat you senseless for offering yourself to Penhammond like a fat Christmas goose."

Eleanor, being Eleanor, was moved to protest. Again, Exmoor stopped her with swift, hard kisses.

"Not. One. Word."

He dragged off her headdress and thrust a hand through her loosely braided hair to hold her anchored. As if she could escape his ravaging mouth! As if she would!

She gloried in the weight that crushed her into the straw.

Reveled in feel of his other hand against her throat.

And burned with raw, unfettered hunger when he yanked down both the bodice of her linen under shift and square neckline of her gown. The silver chain she wore night and day slid to one side as his mouth traced a fiery path from her throat to her breasts. Pinned against the lumpy pallet, Eleanor couldn't rise up to offer him more. Just gasp when he used his teeth and tongue to lave a nipple and bolts of pleasure shot straight from her breast to her belly. He tortured one, then the other, until she was a writhing mass of incoherent need.

Nor did she protest when he reached down to pull up her skirts. The memory of the mindless pleasure he'd given her that night in the garden blazed through her head. Followed hard by the memory of his bitter self-disgust afterward for having come so close to dishonoring them both.

Oh, God. Oh, God.

She would spend endless time in purgatory for this wanton need for release. But she couldn't, *wouldn't* let him damn his eternal soul.

"Hugh!"

It was a groan, a plea.

"Hugh! Please!"

He mistook her hoarse cry. "Aye," he growled. "I will please you. But this time I will please us both."

"Stop!" Desperate to save him from himself, she shoved at his shoulder. "I don't want this. You must stop!"

He went still. He was a dead weight atop her. His manhood as hard and unyielding as a battering ram. Then a shudder passed through him. Slowly, carefully, as if nursing a raw wound, he rolled onto his side.

Eleanor scrambled up on one elbow and poured out her heart. "I have no shred of pride left. Although I think you already know, I confess freely that I love you with all my soul. Too much to allow you to risk yours by foreswearing your sacred vows."

The rigid line to his mouth relaxed and, much to her astonishment, his lips tipped into a sardonic smile. "You make this confession at a most awkward moment, woman."

She didn't need to see the still bold bulge in his chausses to grasp his meaning. "I know, I know. It's as painful for me as it is for you."

"I take leave to doubt that. But let me set your mind at ease." The smile faded, replaced by a dead seriousness. "Taking you outside the bounds of marriage is a mortal sin. One I'll do penance for. It will not, however, cause me to foreswear a sacred vow."

"But.... But Catherine. You're bound to her."

"No longer."

"What? Dear God! She didn't take some accident, did she? She's not dead? Please! Tell me she's not dead!"

The straw rustled as he sat up and took the hands she'd clasped together in distress and dismay. "No, you chucklehead, she didn't have an accident. But when we met on the road to Saint Swithin's and I saw the courage she can never seem to summon around me, I knew I had to end her misery. In the brief moments we had to converse, I told her I would release her and..."

"Hugh! You will not send her back to her father! You cannot!"

"*Jesu*, will you let me finish?"

"Finish, then," she snapped, "and stop nattering on like a witless dolt."

From the way his eyes widened, Eleanor guessed that few people, if any, would dare to call the lord of Exmoor a witless dolt. He took his revenge by knocking her elbow out from under her, toppling her onto back, and pinning her under him again.

"I will tell you, you noisome fishwife, if you will shut your mouth for half a moment."

She matched him stare for stare, then clamped her lips together. Exmoor waited a long, exasperating moment before continuing.

"I told Catherine I would release her from her vows and send her dower back to her father."

Eleanor stiffened in involuntary protest but somehow managed to swallow her outrage.

"Wise," Exmoor commented, observing her struggle. "Very wise."

She was sorely tempted to smack his infuriating face. With another monumental effort, she refrained.

"To repeat, I told Catherine I would release her from her vows and return her dower to her father. And if she agreed to release me, as well, I promised to dower her myself with enough lands and monies to set her up well with Broadsfield."

"Harald?" The air left Eleanor's lungs in a whoosh. "You knew that he…?"

"Christ's bones! Anyone with eyes could see the mooncalf was besotted with her. And she, I thought, with him."

"You *thought?*"

"Aye."

He framed her face with his hands, frowning as he admitted a truth that seemed to be wrenched out of him. "Catherine would not have young Harald."

"What? I thought… I was sure…"

"As was I. But instead, Catherine begged me to dower her sufficiently to endow a nunnery…to which she would retire."

"Ohhh."

Eleanor wanted to grieve for a young girl determined to shut herself away from the world but knew in her heart Catherine had chosen the best course for her. She was so devout, so pious - and so terrified of the very thought of marriage - she would only find surcease from that fear as the bride of Christ.

"Did you agree?" Eleanor asked softly.

"I did."

"Oh, Hugh." Her heart melting, she laid her palm against his cheek. "For Catherine's sake, I thank you."

He gave an inelegant snort and moved on top of her, shifting her attention instantly to the fact that she lay under his hard, unyielding body.

"It's not thanks I want from you, wench."

The bulge was still there. Pressing into her stomach. Setting the torch again to a lust made even more fierce by all he'd just related.

"Oh, so?" she retorted, already breathless. "And are you so disposed to take what you want?"

"Aye, I am."

The kiss was as rough as the one before, and even more demanding. When he raised his head, Eleanor's heart catapulted from all the emotions assaulting it. But he resisted when she locked her arms around his neck and would have pulled his mouth to hers once more.

"Before we go further," he growled, "did I mishear your confession some moments ago? Was that love you spoke of?"

"It was." She was beyond shame, beyond restraint. "I love you to the moon and the stars and all the heavens. You're the one I crossed an ocean to find."

He framed her face in his hands. "And you are the mate I didn't know I was waiting for. I will have you, Eleanor. Now, and always."

Unbidden, the queen's words leaped into her mind. *She would think on a suitable match. She would discuss it with her son. Betimes, she would take Eleanor into her keeping.*

"Hugh…"

"Quiet, fishwife, and let me pleasure you the way a woman with your fire should be pleasured."

Since he'd returned his attention to her breasts and was already stoking the aforementioned fire, she acquiesced. She would relate the queen's edict later. After she and Hugh had satisfied the hunger that had consumed them for so many weeks.

She refused to acknowledge, even to herself, the grim possibility that this might well be the *only* chance they'd have to assuage that hunger. The queen would be most displeased if and when she learned of this forbidden tyst. And not only did the risk her anger. With Marcher lords caught between ever shifting loyalties, Hugh might yet come down on the wrong side of the new king. If that happened, Richard Lionheart would *not* be disposed to give Eleanor and her king's ransom in jewels to an enemy.

No! She would not think of kings and queens and warring border lords now. These stolen moments belonged to Hugh. Only to Hugh.

So when he shoved up her skirts and found her most private place, she raised her hips to give him better access. And when his thumb pressed the throbbing flesh at her core, she gave herself over to the waves of sensation that washed through her.

The waves were still surging, falling, surging again, when he withdrew his hand. And when she moaned an inarticulate protest, he gave a short, hoarse laugh.

"Wait, fishwife. Wait. I but loosen my braes."

She felt his hand fumbling between them. Afire with need, she reached down to help him. He brushed her hand away, kneed her legs further apart and resettled his weight. She could feel him probe at the juncture to her thighs. Feel the slow, deliberate intrusion. She gulped as he probed deeper, then gave a startled cry when he pushed into her.

Surprise held her stiff and still for a moment. Hugh didn't move, either, waiting for her to adjust to the feel of this…this sausage inside her. While her body absorbed the shock, Eleanor's always active mind raced.

How strange! How very surprising! The pain of breaching she'd heard so many married women whisper about had been no worse than pricking her finger with a needle. Quickly come, quickly gone.

Mayhap she'd breached her maiden's shield herself. She'd heard that riding hard in the saddle could do that. If she had, would Hugh believe her a virgin?

Hard on that thought came another. She couldn't help but remember the small, folded square of linen Lady Alice had pressed on her. Almost as soon as it surfaced, she thrust the thought away. Whatever became of her, whatever side of the looming war she and Hugh might land on, she would *never* resort to the mix of powdered pomegranate, juniper and rue that might keep his seed from quickening in her womb.

She was still lost in that fierce vow when he began to move. In. Out. In. Out. Slowly, so slowly, at first. Then faster. Harder. Deeper. Until the waves began to surge again.

She had no way of knowing how many minutes - hours? - passed until those waves swept her up, up, cresting high, tossing her wildly, then slamming into her with such shattering force that she arched her back and gave a long, guttural groan.

His jaw set, Hugh stayed stiff and unmoving while shudders wracked her. Only when they'd subsided did he begin to move again.

She was so tight. So wet. So much a woman. He would say a thousand *pater nosters*. Spend countless hours on his knees. Endow a nunnery or abbey in her name. But he was damned if he would regret the feel of her, the scent of her, the heat of her. She filled him, even more than he now filled her.

And when he spilled his seed into her, he vowed fiercely that he would not let her go to another husband whatever the new king or old queen decreed.

He recovered slowly, waiting for the blood that had drained from his head to return to his outer extremities before he rolled onto his side and brought her into the circle of his arm.

Her head cradled on his shoulder, Eleanor heaved a long sigh before breaking the lingering haze of pleasure. "The queen offered to take me in her keeping. Jasmine and me both."

"God help the royal household."

She balled a fist and punched his ribs. "Jasmine is just a child. Somewhat impetuous, I admit, but…"

"Ha!" He grabbed her fist before she could plough into his ribs again. "That *child* is an unbridled, unrepentant bundle of mischief."

"Much like your brother!"

"I cannot argue that. I only hope neither one of them sets another goat shed or hen house afire before we return to Exmoor."

She nestled her head back on his shoulder and spoke so quietly he had to strain to hear her.

"I won't be returning to Exmoor. Not with you, at any rate. The queen's offer to take Jasmine and me in keeping was most kind and generous, but she cloaked it in a royal command. I'm to accompany her when she leaves tomorrow."

"The devil you say!"

He sat up so abruptly he almost tumbled Eleanor off the pallet. A swift lunge brought him to his feet.

"We'll waste no time, then," he said as he pulled up and retied his braes before shoving his shirt tails into them and buckling on his belt. "We leave now."

"Hugh! We can't defy the queen."

"We can, and we will."

He reached down and dragged her up. Halfway to the door, she set her feet and yanked free of his hold.

"Wait! I can't go anywhere with my bodice all asunder and my hair tumbling down my back like some lowborn wench you've just taken to the straw."

Hugh didn't think it wise to tell her she was the most seductive wench, low- or highborn, he'd ever taken to the straw. Bridling his impatience, he waited for her to tidy herself as best she could, then hustled her through the door.

Once in the shadowed hall, he made a quick decision. He couldn't risk going back to rouse his men and alert the others sheltering at the abbey of their departure. He and Eleanor would have be away now, with only the clothes on their backs. But first, he would retrieve his mail and sword. As dictated by the laws of sanctuary, all men surrendered their arms before being allowed into the abbey. The weaponry was held at the gate house, Hugh knew. And their mounts would be in the stables.

"This way."

His hold still tight on Eleanor's elbow, he steered her down a dark, shadowed corridor and tried to guess the time. Monks went to bed early, just after dusk summer and winter. It was well past that now.

They got up again to sing Nocturns and Lauds, however. To make sure no slackers remained abed, a brother would make rounds with a lamp or candle to check the cells. It was past the hour for Nocturns but wasn't yet midnight, Hugh guessed. Well before Lauds. Still, as he traversed another long, echoing hall, he kept a close watch for any distant glow that might signal a brother making his rounds.

His luck held. He and Eleanor made it to the heavily barred door sealing pilgrims, guests, and monks alike in the refectory for the night. It cost him a pang - and added to the growing list of penances he would have to perform - to creep up behind the sleepy brother who was supposed to attend the door and render him unconscious with a swift blow.

When Hugh raised the bar and put a shoulder to the door, the aged panel creaked and groaned like a tormented ghoul. Cursing, he shoved Eleanor through the narrow opening and into the outer yard. With the moonlight to guide them, they raced for the stables. This time Hugh took pity on the stable hand they startled awake. He spun what sounded even to his own ears like an impossibly implausible tale about an imminent attack on Exmoor and the need to return immediately.

The man was obviously slow-witted. Mouth open, he gawked at the tale but, thankfully, led Hugh to the stalls that housed Sirocco and the other mounts from Exmoor. The stallion recognized Hugh with a toss of his head. Eleanor he greeted with a joyful nicker.

She shushed him by stroking his neck and whispering in his ear while Hugh and the sable hand retrieved saddles and barding. They saddled Sirocco and brought out a bay with long, lean lines, also quickly saddled.

Then Hugh rounded to the stallion's side and cupped his hands. "Mount, fishwife, and let's be away."

Her face lit up, for all the world as if she were embarking on a grand adventure instead of stealing away from a queen in the dead of night. Putting her foot in his hands, she let him toss her into the saddle.

They rode for the remainder of the night and well past dawn, stopping only to rest and water the horses. Hugh already had the measure of the woman he was now determined to claim as his own. But that wild ride added even more to her worth in his eyes.

She never complained. Never begged even a brief rest. And when at last the watchtowers of Exmoor appeared in the distance, she turned to him with a broad grin.

"Well, we've made good our escape. What in the name of God and all the saints do we do next?"

He met her grin with a wide one of his own. Kings, queens, and the fates be damned. "We summon my mother, my brother, my sisters, and my no-longer betrothed to the chapel. They can act as witnesses while Father Anselem joins us."

"And *my* sister. We cannot forget Jasmine."

Would that they could, Hugh thought sardonically as they spurred toward the keep. If he survived the queen's wrath and that of the king for snatching such a rich prize from their hands, he suspected Jasmine would contrive to make his life a holy hell.

Chapter Fourteen

Alerted by the sentries, Sir Giles notified Lady Alice that her son had been spotted. She rushed out to the bailey to greet him. Half the residents of the keep accompanied her, including those tourney guests who'd not yet departed. Their questions flew fast and furious as Hugh dismounted and Eleanor slid as supple as a willow from Sirocco's back.

"How did you manage it?"

"Is it true you met the queen on your way to Saint Swithin's?"

"Did you cleave Penhammond's skull?"

That came from Guy, who looked both disappointed and disapproving when Hugh shook his head.

"What's this Catherine tells us about sending her dower back to her father?" his lady mother asked sharply.

Hugh's glance found the girl he'd considered his intended wife these past years. To his relief, she appeared none the worse for her ordeal. Just the opposite, in fact. Her expression of clumsily suppressed joy, overlaid with outright adoration, made Hugh snort under his breath. The hasty promise he'd made to release her from her betrothal vows had obviously transformed him from dreaded husband to savior.

"We've ridden long and hard," he said to the assembled crowd. "We'll answer your questions while we break our fast. But first I must speak with Father Anselem."

The crowd broke and headed for the inner bailey. Hugh hung back for a private word with his chief vassal. "You'd best post additional sentries on the walls."

"I already have," Sir Giles confirmed. "And I've sent scouts to watch all approaches. We'll hear immediately if they sight a troop headed our way."

"Good man."

Once inside the great hall, he found his mother had issued orders like a battlefield commander.

"The servants are carrying heated water abovestairs for you and Eleanor to wash away your road dirt," she informed him. "They'll bring meats and bread as well. And I've sent word to Father Anselem, requesting he attend you when he's finished the little prayers at Terce."

The "little" prayers at Terce, Sext, and None were said privately and took only moments. So Hugh wasn't surprised when the castle priest rushed into the lord's chamber before Hugh had done more than splash water on his face and hands.

"Were you in time to stop the Lady Eleanor's marriage to Penhammond?"

"I was."

The priest crossed himself with a fervent, "Thanks be to God!"

"But I wish you to conduct another, and quickly."

"To formally join you and Lady Catherine? But I thought… I heard rumors…"

"The rumors are true. Catherine and I have agreed to release each other from our vows and will so swear in front of you and the necessary number of witnesses. I will need you to write a writ of *quidquid voverat atque promiserat.*"

"Hugh! I don't have authority to declare your vows null and void! Such a writ must come from a bishop."

"The office of the Bishop of Chester is vacant."

"Yes, yes, but it can only be a matter months, mayhap weeks, before the Holy Father names a new bishop."

"I don't have months or weeks. I intend to make Lady Eleanor my wife before Richard arrives in England. And before his mother arrives at Exmoor to take her into keeping," he added grimly.

Frowning, the good father worried the rosary hanging from the belt. The wooden beads clicked and clacked while he pulled his conscience this way and that.

"Given that the bishopric of Chester is indeed vacant," he said finally, "I will pen an edict nullifying your betrothal vows. First I must hear you both repudiate them, aloud and before witnesses."

"We'll do so within the hour."

"But be warned, my son. Catherine's father may well challenge my authority to do this in an ecclesiastic court."

"He won't."

"How can you be sure?"

"I'm returning Catherine's dower, and adding twice its worth from my own coffers if he agrees to let her enter a nunnery."

"My lord!" The priest displayed a swift parade of emotions, chief among them profound relief. "I don't break the seal of the confessional when I tell you that a nunnery is what Catherine has long prayed for. But I fear such a heavy sum to win your release will beggar you."

"Not quite. Lady Eleanor brings a dowry almost as rich."

"Ahhhh, yes. The rubies. If the one she gave me to buy alms for the poor is any indication of their worth, they're of great value indeed."

Assuming, Hugh thought, the king allowed him to keep both his bride and her dowry. "We need to perform the marriage this morn, Father. Queen Eleanor may even now on her way to Exmoor."

"God and all the saints help us!" The priest crossed himself again and quickly assessed the possible impediments to such a hurried union. "You and Eleanor are not related within the prohibited degree of kinship and neither of you have taken a vow of celibacy."

Hugh suppressed a smile. He'd confessed his sins often enough for the priest to know celibacy was most definitely not at issue. Nor, obviously, had Eleanor. "We have not."

His mind made up, the priest let his beads drop. "I'll hear you and Catherine repudiate your vows. And I must hear your confession, yours and Eleanor's, before I join you in the sacrament of marriage. Come to the chapel as soon as you're ready. And God help us all," he muttered as he turned to hurry from the chamber.

Freshly bathed and sustained by a quick meal of bread, meats, and ale, Hugh found a host of interested parties clustered together on benches in the great hall.

His mother was there, of course, and Catherine, Sir Giles, his wife Lady Margaret, even young Guy. Adding to their ranks were William Marshal and Ian FitzGilbert, who'd each led patrols to search for Catherine.

"Eleanor sent word she would be downstairs forthwith," his mother informed him. "She wished to, ah, speak with Jasmine in private."

Hugh interpreted that readily enough. The older sister had to convince the younger to take the news that she was about to wed Jasmine's nemesis with at least a show of civility. He didn't hold out much hope Eleanor would succeed.

Jasmine's scowl when she and Eleanor made their appearance a short time later seemed to confirm his worst fears. The girl said nothing, however. Her lips set in mulish lines, she merely sank onto a bench beside Guy and crossed her arms.

As urgent as the moment was, Hugh took some seconds to assess his bride. She showed no evidence of their all-night ride. She'd scrubbed the dirt and fatigue from her face and confined the wild flame of her hair behind a clean wimple and veil. She'd changed her gown, as well. Gone were the shift and bliaut Hugh had all but torn off her. The realization he would soon remove this gown and shift, too, spurred him to action.

Signaling to her to his side, he took her hand in his. "By now you know much of what has happened," he told the small crowd, "but not, mayhap, the details."

He told them of meeting Catherine on her way back to Exmoor. Of their mutual agreement to terminate their betrothal. Of encountering the Queen on the road from Chester and her decision to accompany him to St. Swithin's. And of *his* decision to steal Eleanor out from under the queen's nose and wed her forthwith.

His gaze went to FitzGilbert. The battle-scarred knight took his loss with a resigned shrug. William Marshal, however, gave a long, low whistle.

"You'd best hope you've not made an enemy of the queen. Richard wants only to be crowned, bleed us all dry to fund his Crusade, and be off to the Holy Land. The queen will act as regent in his stead, and her memory is long."

"Long or short, it matters not."

Releasing Eleanor's hand, he went down on one knee beside his betrothed. "Father Anselem is waiting for us to renounce our vows in his presence, Cat. But we do it only if you still wish to. You know I would hold to you, before God and man, should you wish it."

She blushed and stammered but left no doubt of her feelings. "N…no. You've… You've been most kind to me these many years, Hugh. I love you, I truly do. But…not as you love Eleanor and she, you."

He raised her hand to his lips. "I swear on my honor to see you take no harm from this, little mouse."

"I know you will."

"Let's go to Father Anselem, then, and be done with the matter. Sir Giles, will you act as witness?"

"Gladly."

"As will I," William Marshal put in.

"I thank you from my heart," Hugh told his bluff, redoubtable patron, "but I would not have you risk the wrath of the queen by affixing your seal to either the writ dissolving the betrothal vows or the contract of marriage between Eleanor and me."

"Christ's bones, man, I've risked the wrath of the queen and her quarrelsome sons so many times I've lost count. Once more will not matter."

"So be it. Come with me, Cat, and you, Eleanor. We'll dissolve one union, and seal another as soon as Eleanor and I make our confessions."

"You plan to wed now?" his lady mother gasped. "This very morning?"

"This very morning."

"Holy Mother of God!" She sprang off the bench. "I have to ready a wedding feast, or as near to one as we can throw together. Guy! Tell the fowlers I want every bird they have dressed. And instruct John Pigman to bring two of his largest smoked hams to the kitchen sheds. You, Jasmine, gather a basket of pears from the orchard. Lady Margaret, I need as many pies as you and the rest of the ladies can roll out. I'll go down to the spice room now cinnamon and cloves and currants. And nutmeg. We'll need nutmeg."

She started off, swung back in a flurry of skirts and pointed a stern finger at her son. "Get you to Father Anselem, Hugh, and be sure you do every penance he gives you. You as well, Eleanor. But do not *dare* exchange vows until I and the rest of your family have assembled in the chapel."

His voice strong and unwavering, Hugh stated before the assembled witnesses that he had not consummated his marriage to Catherine of Langmont and desired his promise to do so be declared null and void. He also swore to return her dowery to her father.

Pale but determined Catherine swore in a near whisper that she was yet a virgin. Her voice and her courage gained strength, however, when she said that she, too, wished their vows be voided.

Father Anselem produced the parchment he'd hurriedly penned. Hugh signed it and affixed his seal. Then Catherine made her mark and affixed hers. Before leaving the chapel, she kissed both Hugh and Eleanor and wished them a happy life together. The witnesses departed with her, after which it was time for Father Anselem to hear Eleanor and Hugh's confessions.

She squirmed when she confessed that she'd yielded to carnal lust and fornicated with Hugh. To her relief, the priest didn't adhere to the law that required clergy to report known fornicators to justicars, who might punish them with fines or public whippings or days in the stocks. Thankfully, Father Anselem supported the most commonly suggested solution of marriage between the two offenders. Not that he let her off with a light penance, though. Especially after she admitted their fornication took place within the walls of an abbey! She was instructed do the Stations of the Cross. Thrice. In her shift. On her knees.

Hugh's confession took considerably longer. So did his penance. He disappeared from the keep for more than two hours. When he returned, barefoot and drenched from head to toe, he took time only to change his raiment before sending a page to tell Eleanor he awaited her in the chapel.

By then the keep buzzed with activity, and tantalizing aromas of roast duck and fresh baked pies wafted through every hall. As Eleanor approached the chapel, Jasmine's hand held firmly in hers, the headier scent of frankincense greeted her. The sweet, woody fragrance brought a sudden memory of the distant land where she and her sister had both been born and bred.

Jasmine caught the scent, too. She stopped dead, sniffed the fragrant air, and lifted worried eyes to her sister. "Do you really truly want this, Ella? It's not too late. We could still go home."

"No, sweeting, we can't. There's nothing in the East for us any more."

"But... But you don't have to marry Hugh if you don't wish to. Just delay an hour. Two. I can find herbs to give him a bloody flux of the bowels. Or sing an incantation, and mayhap a jinii will carry him off."

"Jasmine! Please! No herbs. No incantations."

Eleanor sank to her knees and folded the girl she'd raised from a babe into her arms. How to make her understand that what she felt for the lord of Exmoor in no way lessened what she felt for this prickly desert flower?

"Hugh holds my heart in his hands, my sweet. Or as much of it that you don't hold in yours. Please, try to love him for my sake."

A small, slipped foot tapped the floor. The slight figure in her arms remained stiff and unyielding for two heartbeats. Three.

"I'll try."

Realizing that grudging promise was the best she could hope for, Eleanor pushed to her feet. "Thank you. Now let's do what we traveled all the way from Outremer to do."

The wedding Mass was both solemn and joyous. The banquet afterward a true testament to Lady Alice. She'd marshaled her kitchen forces like a battlefield commander. Everyone seated above and below the salt praised her skills as minstrels sang, wine and ale flowed, and course followed course. Eleanor did full justice to a hearty pottage, followed by pheasant stuffed with oysters and walnuts, smoked ham baked with wild mushrooms in elaborate puff pastries, turnips stewed with onions and carrots, and fresh caught salmon from the River Alyn.

By the time servers paraded platters of savories and fruit tarts and sugared pastries, more than three hours had passed. Eleanor was seated beside Hugh and couldn't help but note his frequent exchange of glances with Sir Giles.

They expected the queen at any time, mayhap with Penhammond's men to augment her own. So Eleanor made no demur when her groom announced that he and his bride were retiring.

Raucous jests filled the air, followed bawdy toasts that shocked Catherine, brought a frown to Lady Alice, and made Eleanor laugh. She was still chuckling when she and Hugh gained his chamber, thankfully empty of all other occupants.

"You continue to amaze me, lady wife. Those crude jests would put most women to the blush."

"Most women did not grow from girlhood with a sire such as mine."

"You'll have to tell me more of him. Later."

Since he'd already reached up to remove the circlet anchoring her gossamer veil, she voiced no objection to the delay. The veil fell away, then the pins that held her braided coronet. Smiling, he undid the thick braid and combed his fingers through the strands.

"This was the first I saw of you. The day you came to Exmoor. You were astride Sirocco, bent low over his neck, and your veil flew off. Your unbound hair flamed in the sun."

Eleanor had to laugh. "And when first I saw you, husband, I mistook you for a stablehand."

Those eyes, those wondrous blue eyes, lost their smile. "I will not give you up without a fight, Eleanor."

"I know."

"But the fight may come sooner rather than later. We may not have much time together."

"I know that, too." Impatiently, she tugged at the ties to his shirt. "So why do we waste it?"

With that grim prediction to spur them, she expected their joining to be swift, Urgent. What she didn't expect was the slow, tantalizing way Exmoor removed her garments. One after another, they dropped to the woven carpet to join her discarded veil. The wide girdle that circled her hips. The square-necked bliaut with sleeves so long they tipped the floor. The linen shift so painstakingly and richly embroidered at neck and hem. Even her ribboned garters, stockings, and slippers, until she stood before him in nothing but her silver chain with its little key.

Eleanor knew she should feel shame. Shield her breasts and loins. The summer sun still blazed bright, for pity's sake! Birds still twittered. And everyone belowstairs knew exactly what they were about.

Yet all that gripped her was the driving need to bare him, as he'd bared her. She was less adept in the disrobing, however. He'd left off his chain mail and padded gambeson, choosing to wear only a fur-trimmed mantle emblazoned with Exmoor's golden eagle, but he had to stoop for her to pull it over his head. She managed to remove his linen under shirt but swore when she mangled the ties on his drawers.

"Let me," he said, brushing her hands aside.

While he worked the ties, Eleanor's hungry gaze roamed his naked chest. The roped muscles didn't surprise her. Or the bruises and faded scars. He was a battle-tested warrior, after all, and had just competed in a melee. But when he bent to pull off his woolen stockings, the vicious bruise slashing across the back of his neck made her gasp.

"Sweet Virgin above, Hugh! That looks as though you came near to having your head separated from your shoulders."

"I did, but I parried the blow before it cut through my neck guard and took Penhammond down before he could swing again."

"Penhammond did that?"

Holy Mary! Their enmity ran deeper than Eleanor had realized. The certainty that it wouldn't end until one of them was dead settled in her stomach like a stone.

Exmoor read the dread in her face. As naked as she was now, he curled a finger under her chin and tipped it. "You have nothing to fear from him, Eleanor. I'll grind him into the dirt like the muckworm he is. But first, lady wife…" His hand moved to the curve of her breast. "…we have more important matters to attend to."

Chapter Fifteen

They had three days.

On the first, a rider sent by the Earl of Chester brought word that the queen had cut short her progress and was returning with all speed to Winchester to welcome her son to England and arrange for his coronation.

On the second, William Marshal departed with promises to send men and arms should they be needed.

On the third, they received word that Richard had landed at Portsmouth.

The hours between those momentous events were busy beyond measure. By day, Hugh and Sir Giles saw to the gathering of enough supplies, grains, and livestock to withstand a possible siege. They also requisitioned a good store of pitch to fire and hurl at attackers, as well as tanned hides to soak and drape over wooden structures within the curtain wall to protect them from fire arrow. Water was essential to withstanding a siege, so they set men to digging a second deep well. With those efforts hard afoot, Hugh sent missives to his vassals in England and on the continent to inform them of his marriage to Eleanor de Brac and remind them of their obligation to provide armed troops if and when required.

Eleanor, too, worked tirelessly alongside the other women of the keep. Lady Alice tried to yield her place as chatelaine but her son's new wife demurred, saying she had much to learn yet about ordering the fifty or more cooks and gardeners and candlemakers and other craftsmen and maids who worked and lived within Exmoor's walls. Even more to learn about preparing for a possible siege.

Every hour of those three days flew by, each one busier than the last. But the nights...

Ahhh, the nights. Those belonged to Eleanor and Hugh.

Despite the lingering August heat, they drew the bed hangings when they retired. The others who slept on pallets in various corners and niches of the lord's chamber knew what went on behind the hangings, of course. There was little privacy in any manor or castle.

Yet Eleanor was convinced none of them, not even the long-married couples who shared this, the largest room in the keep aside from the great hall, could have experienced the same wonder, the same delight she did as she came to know her husband's body, muscle by well-honed muscle, kiss by lingering kiss. Hugh conducted the same intimate explorations. If Eleanor had possessed even a shred of maidenly modesty, she would've lost it that first night as his wife.

By the second, she didn't utter so much as a whispered protest when he raised her legs and hooked her knees over his shoulders. What he did to her then *had* to be a sin! She couldn't imagine it was condoned by church, even between husband and wife. And when he used both teeth and tongue to drive her to near madness, he compounded the sin by dragging her back from the edge. Again, and yet again! Until she bit her lip so hard she tasted blood to keep from crying out and waking the others.

"Finish it!" she hissed when she could stand no more. "Damn you to a thousand hells, finish it."

"Oh, no. Not yet."

"Hugh, have pity! I cannot take more!"

"Aye, fishwife, you can."

To prove his point, he lowered her legs and used them as a lever to flip her over. Eleanor felt his hard palm slide under her stomach. The next she knew, she was on her hands and knees.

She had time for only the fleeting thought that this had to be against the laws of both church *and* man before he thrust into her. As wet and ready as she was, this new, shameful, thoroughly erotic position drove her to even more maddening heights.

When at last she collapsed face down onto the thick-stuffed mattress, she was drenched with sweat and so limp she could scarce find the strength to draw a breath. The twisted linen sheets tugged at her belly as Hugh stretched out beside her.

She opened one eye to squint at him. "What we just did must surely condemn us to hell."

"If it does," he replied with a grin that showed white in the darkness, "we'll be keeping company of half the men in Christendom. A good number of their ladies, too."

The mattress sagged as he pushed up on one elbow and reached over to tuck her sweat-dampened hair behind her ear.

"Crusaders have brought back fantastical tales of the, ah, dexterity of the women of the East. Did Jasmine's mother not share any of her secrets with you?"

It took a heroic effort, but Eleanor gathered enough strength to roll onto her side. "She was a slave, and a most surly one at that. I tried to engage her but she would have nothing to do with me."

"Do you know her tribe, or where she was taken?"

"She was Berber. That much I got from her. But little else except a simmering hate for all invaders. In truth, I woke each morning expecting to find she'd slit my father's throat in his sleep and disappeared."

"Why didn't she?"

"I've often puzzled over that. The only explanation I can come up with was that her belly swelled so soon after my father won her. She didn't want to escape while carrying the get of a despised invader. Her tribe would've condemned her, mayhap stoned her. So she waited long months until she dropped the babe, then disappeared that same night. I can only give thanks to God that she didn't strangle the babe."

Hugh huffed. "I think the devil had more to do with it."

Laughing softly, Eleanor traced a finger along her husband's prickly chin. "I know you think Jasmine a hell-born imp. But from the first moment I held her in my arms, she's given me such joy. I can only hope our children have her spirit and brave heart."

"Ha! I'll say a dozen *pater nosters* each morning and night that they do not. But…" He caught the hand still raised to trace his cheeks and chin. "Since we speak of children, you don't want me to commit the added sin of withholding my my seed, do you?"

She feigned horror. "You must do your duty, husband!"

"Then lie back, wife, and do yours."

"Oh, no." With a sly grin, she resisted when he would have rolled her onto her back. "You used me as a stallion uses a mare earlier. Now I've a mind to throw my leg over you and ride you until I've broken you to saddle."

She was accustomed to the darkness enough by now that to see sudden gleam that came into his eyes. "Do you think you can?"

"I do."

Her boast was mostly in jest. She was sure their strenuous activities coming after such a long, labor-filled day had sapped his strength as much as hers. At the most, she anticipated a quick gallop.

Yet even before she settled astride his hips, she felt his staff jerk under her. An instant, answering heat curled through her veins, and her heart began to dance and skip. Gulping, she braced her hands on his sweat-dampened shoulders to take him more fully.

Once seated, she slid her hands down. And down. The hair on his chest felt damp to her touch, his belly was as hard as iron. When she raised up on her knees just enough to circle her fingers around the root of his rod, his entire body went taut.

Grunting, he removed her fingers. "You'd best let me take the reins, or this ride will over before it's begun."

Not the least bit reluctant, she planted her hands on his shoulders again. The move brought her breasts to within a mere inch or two from his mouth.

When Eleanor finally dropped to the sheets again in sheer exhaustion, she did so with the satisfaction of knowing that they'd done their duty as man and wife.

Their coupling on the third night was every bit as exhausting but, for Eleanor at least, driven as much by desperation as need. The confirmation of Richard arrival in England added urgency to her kisses and caresses. But Hugh refused to be rushed. He roused her slowly, deliberately. Touching. Tasting. Mingling their scent, their sweat. As if etching each curve and hollow in his mind. Despite the way his calloused palm set every nerve to tingling, Eleanor could could not free her mind of the worry that plagued her the following morning.

She did her best to hide that worry from others. Particularly Jasmine. Guy had already filled the girl's head with tales of how the as-yet uncrowned king had earned the sobriquet "Lionheart."

Yes, Eleanor had no choice but to confirm, Richard was rumored to be as fearsome as he was fearless in battle.

Yes, he'd rebelled against his father, the king.

Yes, he exacted swift vengeance against the lords who in turned rebelled against him in Anjou, Poitiers, and Normandy.

And yes, he'd would exact vengeance against any English or Welsh lords who dared do the same. But he was anxious to claim his crown and be off on Crusade. Odds were, he would forgive many previous faults and transgressions to make sure he left loyal lords behind.

Eleanor's calm assurances fell on deaf ears. Ever bloodthirsty, Jasmine devised a long list of the ways she could bring this Richard Lionheart to his knees if he posed a threat to Eleanor or Lady Alice or Guy or Catherine. Or, she admitted sourly, even Hugh.

Eleanor was just as unsuccessful at soothing Catherine's worries. The possibility that her father would refuse Exmoor's offer to compensate for repudiating his daughter ranked almost as high as her fear that Richard take a hand in disposing of her person and her rich dowery to another husband. She dissolved into frequent bouts of tears and spent even more hours than before in the chapel. Lady Alice grew so exasperated that she all but banished the girl from her sight.

All Catherine's fears came to a head that very morning. Her cheeks turned ice gray when Hugh told her he'd received an answer to the missive he sent to the Abbess of Cheshire Priory. Founded a few short years after William the Conqueror added England to his vast realm, the Benedictine nuns at Cheshire lived a cloistered life of contemplative silence, continual prayer and good works.

"What... What did the abbess say?"

"That she would be most happy to welcome her into their midst, if you truly wish it."

Bursting into tears, Catherine fell on his chest. "Thank you! Thank you! I've prayed so hard... Tried so hard..."

"I know, Sweet Cat. I know."

He held her close. Although their long betrothal had been dissolved, he still felt a deep affection and ingrained responsibility for the wife he once thought to make his own.

"Are you sure this is what you want, little mouse?"

"Yes." Her head tilted back. Through their sheen of tears, her eyes held a joyous light Hugh had rarely, if ever glimpsed in them. "Oh, yes."

"Then we'd best get you packed and gone to the abbey before…"

"Before Richard or Queen Eleanor get wind of this," she finished with a gulp. "I know you risk their wrath for this, Hugh. And the enmity of my father. He'll snatch at your offer to return twice the dowry I brought to you, all the while complaining that you should pay more. But you have given me the greatest gift of all, one I never hoped to have. I will thank you for it every day that God gives me."

She came up on her toes and kissed him. It was the first kissed she'd ever offered of her own volition. The soft brush of her lips against his cheek banished whatever lingering doubts Hugh might have harbored.

Catherine was still in the process of preparing to depart when a courier rode through the portcullis. The sergeant-at-arms on duty needed only a glance at the coat of arms stitched on the courier's surcoat to recognize those gold lions on their field of red and know the man had come on royal business.

Word of his arrival spread quickly, and brought Catherine flying down from the ladies' bower as though on winged feet. Lady Alice and Eleanor rushed up from the storeroom where they'd been tallying just-delivered barrels of dried herring. Even Father Anselem hurried from the chapel, accompanied by Guy. The latter had, of course, demanded he be released from his lessons when alerted by the clatter of hooves and noisy gathering in the bailey. Jasmine, never far from her boon companion, came hard on Guy's heels.

Lady Alice started to greet the arrivals, then stopped and left it to the lady of the manor. Belatedly recalled to her new responsibilities, Eleanor stepped forward.

"I bid you both welcome in my husband's stead," she told the royal courier. "He has ridden out to inspect one of his manor houses."

In fact, he'd ridden out to insure the manor's steward had received word of Richard's arrival in England and understood that the next days or weeks might prove even more uncertain than normal. The queen's messenger did not need to know that, however.

"We'll send him word of your arrival," Eleanor informed the dusty traveler. "Please, come inside and refresh yourself while you await his return."

As the courier dismounted, Lady Alice and Eleanor shared a speaking look. The arrival of a royal courier rarely boded well for the recipients of their messages.

Thankfully, they didn't have to endure a protracted period of suspense. Hugh strode into the great hall before the turn of the hourglass, his boots muddy and his linen shirt clinging to his chest under his leather jerkin.

"I am Hugh Montmercy, lord of this keep. You have a message for me?"

"I do, lord. I am William de Breque, herald to Eleanor, by the grace of God, Queen of England. She sends you greetings and desires me to deliver you this missive."

When the courier removed a square of folded parchment from the leather pouch belted around his waist, Hugh gave the thick wax seal only a brief glance. "Were you instructed to await a response?"

"Aye, lord. And I'm to return with it as soon as you put quill to parchment."

Eleanor gulped but Hugh merely nodded. "You'll have it within the hour. Guy, go to the stables and make sure his mount is well tended to."

The import of a missive from the queen wasn't lost on any of his household. The joy that had stained Catherine's cheeks a happy pink as she packed for her journey to the priory faded, leaving them pale and her eyes worried. Eleanor and her mother-in-law were no less concerned.

"Lady wife, lady mother, will you accompany me above stairs? And you as well, Father Anselem. I may need another copy of the writ you penned for us some days ago."

Eleanor didn't draw so much as a single breath while Hugh broke the seal, unfolded the parchment, and skimmed the contents. Her stomach dropped like a stone when he relayed them.

"I'm commanded to deliver the lady Eleanor de Brac to the queen's apartments in the Tower of London immediately upon receipt of this letter."

The stark pronouncement produced a fraught silence. His mother broke it with a hiss.

"She calls her Eleanor De Brac. Not 'your lady wife' or 'the lady of Exmoor.' The queen must not know yet that you have wed, Hugh."

"Mayhap. Or mayhap she refuses to recognize the marriage as valid, since we didn't petition the crown for permission to wed."

"Thank the Lord that William Marshal put his seal on the wedding contracts! Neither the queen nor her son can question his honor or the validity of the documents."

Richard shrugged. "We all know how skilled these Plantagenets are at invalidating marriage contracts. I'm also commanded to remain in London for the coronation, then swear allegiance to the new king."

The silence was longer this time and even more ominous. Eleanor had to swallow twice before she could force a quiet question.

"What will we do?"

Her feigned calm belied the tumult raging in her heart. Refusing to obey this royal command would put Hugh squarely on the side of those Marcher lords still debating whether to recognize Richard as king.

All the talk, all the argumentation came down to this moment, this decision. Hugh must now choose whether he would swear for Richard in trade for the king's recognition of this hurried marriage. The thought that he might barter his honor for her was like a spike through Eleanor's chest. In the weeks since she'd arrived at Exmoor, she'd come to admire him greatly for holding so rigidly to that honor. And for keeping his vows to a timid, would-be-bride who blanched every time he addressed her while refusing to repudiate her or send her back to her father.

"Hugh, listen to me," Eleanor pleaded. "The queen's heard rumors of the rubies I brought from the East but she doesn't know about the rest of the baubles in my little casket. No one does, except you and Lady Alice. If Richard's as mad to go on Crusade as all say, mayhap we can buy his approval of our marriage without you having to swear allegiance. Or least buy a little more time until you do."

"I won't rob you of your dower."

She gave a deliberate, derisive snort. "I called you a witless dolt at Saint Swithin's, did I not?"

Lady Alice gasped and Father Anselem frowned, but Hugh's mouth tipped into a wry smile. "Aye, fishwife you did."

"Now I must add prideful and arrogant to witless."

That was too much for his mother. "Eleanor! You shouldn't speak thus to your lord!"

"And so I wouldn't, if he did not deserve it. What good is a dower if it can't buy for me the husband I've already given myself - and my heart - to."

She turned back to Hugh. "Well, husband? Do we refuse the queen's command and prepare for attack? Or do we go to London?"

He pulled in a deep breath, let it out. "We go to London."

"So be it. But when you pen your answer, be sure to tell the queen that you and your *lady wife* will be most pleased to attend her."

Chapter Sixteen

Eleanor fully anticipated the storm Jasmine would raise when told she was to remain at Exmoor while her sister and brother-by-marriage journeyed to London.

The tempest burst as expected. Those emerald eyes, so striking against her desert skin, flashed green fire. Her knuckles showed white where she gripped the hilt of her dagger. With her other hand, she whipped off her veil and threw it to the floor. When she stamped on it with both feet, Eleanor ran out of patience.

"Jasmine! Cease this nonsense! You will stay with Lady Alice until I send for you."

"Pah! I'll not sit sewing altar cloths while you…"

"Heed me! You'll stay if I must lock you in the dungeons."

"You would not."

"I will! Immediately, if you don't stop this caterwauling. Hugh wants to be away within the hour."

"Then be away with you!"

Whirling, she stomped off.

Eleanor resisted the fierce urge to call her back for a kiss and an embrace. God only knew when they'd see each other again. When Jasmine's temper fired, however, it was best to let the flames sputter and die of their own accord.

As it was, Eleanor scarce had time to stuff several changes of linens, two of her best gowns and a selection of wimples and veils into traveling baskets. She then made a quick descent to the counting room with Lady Alice to retrieve her casket. Thrusting the key in the lock, she flipped up the lid. A quick search produced the gold ring with its magnificent emerald.

"In case I don't return, this is to dower Jasmine. And these…"

She pulled out a collar of gold links woven with the same glittering green gem, then pawed through the remaining heap and extracted a girdle of linked silver chains studded with sapphires.

"Please give this to Catherine to offer as a gift to the abbey. It will add to the good will with the abbess when she enters the cloister."

"Indeed, it will." Alice accepted the girdle but refused to acknowledge the possibility Eleanor might be held by the king or queen. "I'll guard the emerald most closely until you can present it to Jasmine yourself."

"Thank you, Lady Alice."

"Lady mother. You must call me lady mother."

Eleanor couldn't remember the last time she'd shed tears. But the gentle reminder that she now had a mother to fill the place of the one she'd never known made her eyes burn.

"You'll need a maid to attend to your needs," the older woman said after she, too, sniffed back tears. "Take Bess. She's young and sometimes silly, but quick and more than passing bright. She'll keep your hair and your gowns in good order."

"Thank you, lady mother. For Bess, and all else you've done for both Jasmine and me. I only pray my sister will not plague you to death while I'm gone."

"I pray so, too."

Her tone suggested she didn't hold out much hope. Nor did Eleanor, but she didn't have time to search for Jasmine and coax her out of her sullens. Still, she wished she could have given her one last word of farewell.

Since they planned to travel fast, Hugh had assembled a troop of only twenty mounted men-at-arms, augmented by Thomas Beckwith, his squire, two pages, and a thoroughly excited young Bess. He also ordered a draught horse instead of oxen to pull the two-wheeled cart carrying the supplies they'd need for the five day journey so as to maintain a quicker pace.

Five hours after departing Exmoor they reached the old Roman road that led from Chester to London. Sirocco tossed his head and gave every sign he wanted to test his legs on the wide, rutted track but Hugh kept him on a short rein.

"Does this really stretch all the way London?" Eleanor asked, marveling at the way the road marched over hills and down dales. "It does. The Romans wanted to connect their capital of Lundinium with the fortress at Chester. That fort and the great wall stretching eastward from it kept the Celtic tribes from sweeping down from the north. Much of both the fortress and wall still stand today."

"The Romans were certainly skilled builders," Eleanor commented. "The fortress Herod erected to protect the second temple still stands in Jerusalem, too. Or did," she amended, "before Saladin took the city and…"

"My lord!"

The shout brought Hugh twisting in his saddle, his hand going instinctively to his sword hilt.

"You'd best come see this," one of the rear guards called.

Wheeling Sirocco, he rode back to where several men-at-arms milled around the now halted supply wagon. Eleanor strained to see what was amiss as Hugh threw back one of the hides covering the supplies. He went rigid in the saddle for several seconds before reaching over the wagon's side. When he plucked out a small, squirming bundle, Eleanor let out a groan.

"Oh, sweet Mother of God!"

His face like a thundercloud, Hugh tucked the wiggling bundle under one arm and rode back to the head of the column. "Did you have aught to do with this, wife?"

"She did not!" The indignant response came from the girl hanging almost upside down over his forearm. "Nor did Guy," she panted. "Craven coward that he is, he refused to even so much as help me devise a way to accompany you."

"Oh, Jasmine…"

With some effort, the girl got a grip on Sirocco's mane and used it to pull herself almost upright. She couldn't escape Hugh's iron hold, however.

"You brute! You bruise my stomach."

"That's not all I intend bruise, you devil's whelp."

"Not here," Eleanor begged. "Not now. Please, Hugh! Send her back to Exmoor. I promise I'll wield a birch rod myself when we return."

If they returned.

She shoved that thought aside and held her breath for long moments while the issue hung in the balance. Finally her still thoroughly irritated husband summoned the captain of his troop.

"Here, take two men with you and return this imp from Hell to Exmoor." With callous disregard for the struggling girl's dignity, he tossed her to the startled captain. "Be warned! If she escapes, you'll be mucking out the stables for the rest of your days."

"She won't, lord."

He settled his indignant charge before him in the saddle and turned his mount. Eleanor had time only to call out a blessing in the tongue of the desert people before Hugh ordered their diminished troop forward.

As the day wore on they encountered more and more travelers. A significant number of the Marcher lords, it seemed, had decided to answer the queen's summons and pledge allegiance to her son. The hold-outs, Hugh related grimly, would find themselves sorely outnumbered.

Weary travelers took shelter in abbeys or keeps when they could and slept in open fields when they could not. On the last day of their journey, Hugh sent the now empty wagon with half his remaining troop back to Exmoor. With such large crowds gathering for the king's coronation, every noble's house would be full to overflowing. As would every inn and alehouse and stable.

The question of where she and Hugh would be housed gnawed at Eleanor. He'd been ordered to deliver her to the queen's apartments in the Tower. Yet even Eleanor, born and raised so far distant from London, knew the grim fortress housed royal prisoners as well as royal residents. Her father had shared many a tale of high-born lords who'd been rowed in through the Tower's water gate, never to be seen again,

Her worry mounted with each mile closer to London but was temporarily shoved aside when they reached the city itself. Entering via the Watling Gate, they wound through a bewildering maze of foul smelling streets crowded with wooden shops and dwellings. The structures' upper stories leaned so close together that Eleanor guessed the occupants could reach out and touch hands. And, as she quickly discovered, the overhangs presented a real hazard to those who didn't leap aside quickly at the warning shout of, "'Ware."

They reached the Tower without a noxious dousing from a chamber pot, thanks be to God. But when the square, solid fortress loomed before them, Eleanor's dread returned full force. So much so that her stomach tied itself in knots as they waited in the outer bailey while a guardsman delivered word of their arrival.

A seneschal wearing royal livery appeared after a nerve-twisting time. "The queen and her retinue have moved to Westminster Palace in preparation for her son's coronation," he informed them. "She left word that you should attend her at Westminster, Sir Hugh. You, and your lady wife have been assigned lodgings there."

Eleanor waited only until they'd ridden back through the Tower gate to gasp in relief. "She knows! Hugh, the queen knows we're wed."

"So it appears."

"And we're not to lodged in the Tower! That betokens well, does it not?"

"We'll know soon enough."

By they time they joined the flow of riders, carriages, litters and drays on the Strand, purple and gold streaked the sky. The great manses lining the thoroughfare already blazed with light at their many windows, and Eleanor caught glimpses of lamplit barges and water boats plying the Thames beyond.

Her nerves balled into a knot again as the spires and turrets of Westminster Palace hove into view. But when their cavalcade rode into the palace's vast courtyard, the whirlwind of activity once again roused her lively curiosity. They were greeted with the news that the coronation would take place just two days hence, and they were among the last wave of arrivals.

Despite her nervousness, Eleanor couldn't help but be awed by the Westminster's immense facade. She was still taking in its magnificence when a young knight wearing royal livery came hurrying in response to the groom sent to announce their arrival.

"I bid you and your lady welcome, Sir Hugh. I am Guy d'Iberville, one of the queen's *valet de chambres*. If you will come with me, I will show you to the place set aside for you."

"I would know first where my men will be bedded down."

"We've put up tents in the fields just beyond the west courtyard, lord. You men will find adequate shelter there, as well as pasturage for the horses. But this one...." He ran an admiring eye over Sirocco's sleek lines. "I'm sure the grooms can find a place for him in the royal stables."

"I prefer he go with my men. They'll tend to him."

Eleanor didn't have to guess at Hugh's reasoning. He want his troop and their mounts together, in one place, should they have to make a quick departure.

With a droll glance at Eleanor, Hugh instructed his sergeant to groom Sirocco well. "He especially likes to have his legs rubbed with weven hay."

"Aye, lord."

Hugh's squire, the two pages, and young Bess toted the panniers containing their belongings as d'Iberville led them though the palace's massive central entrance. Westminster's facade was awe-inspiring enough. But its great hall stole Eleanor's breath.

The vast interior seemed to stretch forever. Two rows of pillars marched the length of the hall, dividing it into thirds. A hundred or more tall windows now purpled with dusk graced one side of the hall. Gloriously embroidered tapestries interspersed with elaborate coats of arms and displays of weaponry decorated the opposite wall. Torches set in iron holders ran the whole length of the hall, and the center nave boasted three impossibly long tables even now being set for the evening meal by a battalion of scurrying servants.

Eyes wide, Eleanor craned her neck to examine a ceiling that rose so high she could barely see its carved rafters. When d'Iberville noted her stunned reaction to the hall's sheer immensity, he puffed with pride. "It's the largest in all Christendom, lady. The length of four jousting fields. William Rufus - the son of William the Conqueror - wanted to impress his subjects and guests with its power and majesty."

It certainly impressed Eleanor. So did the elegantly dressed men and women gathered in knots in the many alcoves formed by the rows of pillars. Their chatter echoed in the vast space, adding to the thumps and clatters of platters and drinking vessels being set out for the evening meal.

"You've not much time to refresh yourself before the trumpets sound the call to dinner," d'Iberville warned as he wove a path through the milling groups. "Barely enough time to find your chamber and wash off your travel dust."

Duly warned, Hugh exchanged only brief greetings with the various lords who hailed him and promised to speak with several at length later. The few cautious exchanges told Eleanor as plainly as words that they, too, were as yet unsure of where they would stand with the new king.

When d'Iberville led them through a side door and down a series of halls, Eleanor paid special attention to their direction. Or tried to. She was soon lost beyond measure.

"This palace is like a city unto itself!" she exclaimed. "How many rooms are there?"

"More than a thousand. I confess I still get lost at times," the *valet de chambres* said with a grin. "If you do, just request one of the maids or valets to direct you."

Given swarm of lords and ladies who'd been in the great hall, Eleanor expected she and Hugh would have to share a crowded chamber with a half dozen or more of their peers. To her relief, d'Iberville informed them that the small side chamber assigned to them would house only one other lord, his lady, and their attendants.

The other occupants were just preparing to exit chamber when the newcomers arrived. The lord was tall and well dressed and sported a wiry bush of whiskers on each cheek.

"Montmercy!" Striding forward, he gave Hugh a kiss of greeting. "I wondered if you would answer the queen's call."

"I wondered the same of you, Fulk."

"Christ knows, I debated long and hard. But we'll leave such talk for later," he said without sending the queen's man so much as a sideways glance. "First, make me and my lady known to yours."

Eleanor had time to form only a fleeting impression of Fulk's stout, merry-cheeked wife before d'Iberville reminded them again that they all must needs repair to the great hall in short order. That prompted a flurry of unpacking by Thomas Beckwith, the two pages and young Bess. With a tapestried screen to offer privacy, Eleanor and Hugh swiftly shed their travel-stained clothing, washed away their road dirt, and changed into finer garments.

Eleanor's gown was the most elegant she possessed. Cut square at the neck and trimmed with snowy miniver, the seagreen bliaut boasted sleeves so long the tasseled tips dragged the floor. She covered her braided hair with a veil of shimmering, pale green silk woven by nimble fingers in a faraway land. When she anchored it with a gold circlet studded with pearls, Fulk's plump little lady breathed an envious sigh. "Oh, Lady Eleanor. You look like a princess."

"S'truth!" Her husband agreed. "Much like the queen when she was as young and beautiful. She'll see herself in you, Lady Eleanor, bless my bones if she won't."

Eleanor hoped so! Mayhap the queen would then accept the need that had driven her to take Hugh to husband, much like the need that had driven the queen herself to take a lusty young second husband mere weeks after the Pope granted an annulment of her first marriage.

That time was long past, of course. And the passion that had produced eight children had died a painful death during the queen's long years of imprisonment. But memories of it, and of happier times, still lived within her. Eleanor had heard an echo of them in the queen's voice during their brief colloquy at St. Swithin's. Had seen it in the way her thoughts turned inward and brought a fleeting smile to her lips.

Would God that the queen held to those memories!

"Are you ready, wife?"

She summoned a bright, determined smile. "I am, husband."

Before they departed, Hugh issued a last, low-voiced command to his squire. "You or one of the pages must stay within this chamber at all times. Guard the casket wrapped inside Lady Eleanor's fox trimmed mantle well."

"And so we will, lord."

Chapter Seventeen

The several hundred lords who'd answered the queen's summons sat shoulder-to-shoulder and hip-to-hip alongside their ladies at long tables groaning with every imaginable fruit of the realm. Hugh's rank relative to the great archbishops, dukes, and earls in attendance placed him and Eleanor above the salt, but barely. Fulk and his lady were seated across from them. Even before Eleanor wedged onto the bench beside Hugh, her every sense was assaulted by the near-shouted conversations, the unceasing clatter of bowls and platters, and the cloying, almost overpowering musk of bodies crammed too close together on this, the first night of September.

Oh, but the elegance! Jewels circled the ladies' throats and studded the gold chains draped across their lords' chests. Veils shimmered and circlets glittered with precious gems. The men's caps sported tassels and broaches and, in several eye-catching instances, peacock plumes.

Gold plate and Venetian goblets rimmed with gold added to the opulence. She was still admiring the goblets' artistry when trumpets sounded and the queen swept in to take her place at the high table. With her, Eleanor saw on a swift indrawn breath, was a most familiar figure.

"Hugh! It's William Marshal. What tipped his decision to come, do you think?"

"The queen, I would guess. I suspect she promised that she would convince her son to honor Marshal's betrothal to Isobel de Clare."

Eleanor sent up a fervent prayer that that the queen would sway her son in their favor, too, as other lords took their places at the high table. Among them was a dark-visaged, unsmiling prince who could only be Richard's last surviving brother, the Count of Morain. Or John Lackland, as he was often labeled. The only of the Henry and Eleanor's five sons who couldn't lay claim to a dukedom. Rumor was he fiercely coveted Richard's lands and titles, and that the queen would need to keep the younger son on a tight rein when the elder left on Crusade. Richard himself, however, made no appearance.

"He'll spend these last days before his coronation at the Tower," Hugh explained, "being shriven of his sins and doing penance for them."

Eleanor thought he must have committed a veritable mountain of sins if they required two full days and nights of confession and penance. His pledge to take up the Cross and go on Crusade must surely have given him a goodly measure of absolution, though.

As expected, the Crusade dominated conversation through most of the long, elaborate meal. The men were especially eager to hear news of Fredrick Barbarossa's progress. The German king, better known as the Holy Roman Emperor, had set out on in May with an army of some fifteen thousand men. Advance contingents of Richard's vassals in Normandy and Anjou had begun departing, as well. Some had joined forces with Barbarossa to help King Sancho of

Portugal conquer the Moorish city of Silves in Iberia. From there, they'd continued their journey to the Holy Land.

King Phillip of France, too, had gathered his vast army and was ready to depart. He waited only for Richard and the bulk of English forces to join him. Small wonder the renowned warrior who'd earned the name Lionheart for his fearlessness in battle chafed at the delay necessitated by his coronation.

There was much discussion of whether Richard would issue the same edicts Fredrick Barbarossa had regarding the Jews.

"The Emperor put the Jews under his protection," a lord newly arrived from the continent for the coronation related. "Small wonder," he added dryly, "considering the monies they've contributed to his war chest."

"Is it true Barbarossa has even forbidden the Church to preach against them?" another asked.

"It is indeed."

This caused no little muttering. Unsurprising, given that generations of Frankish lords had sacrificed much in their repeated attempts to free the Holy Land from "non-believers". And, Eleanor knew, because so many of these same lords owed vast sums to Jewish merchants and money-lenders. As she'd related to Hugh, she'd gained more than a passing familiarity with such matters due to her father's easy-going but sadly profligate ways.

She said nothing during the discussion, however, well aware that a woman's views would hold little credit with these strangers. Only after the banquet did she ask Hugh whether he thought Richard would follow Barbarossa's lead in the matter.

"I have no doubt he will. Jews have held a vital place in banking and finance in England since the time of William the Conqueror. Under Richard's father, Henry II, they prospered greatly. One, Aaron of Lincoln, is reputed to be among the richest men in all of England."

"But I heard much grumbling at dinner."

"Aye, the fall of Jerusalem and the loss of so many Christians during the Crusades have since turned many against them. They still hold vast wealth, though. And Richard is so anxious be crowned and be gone, I don't doubt he'll drain their coffers in return for extending them royal protection."

As, Eleanor feared, he would drain Hugh's. She spent so long on her knees that night, praying for the king's forbearance, that her husband had dozed off by the time she crawled in beside him. He woke quickly enough, though, and drew the coverlet over their heads so he could have his way with her.

The summons from the queen came early, just after morning Mass. Hugh was to attend her alone, unaccompanied the woman who'd shown herself so ungrateful for the queen's offer of protection.

"Take the casket," Eleanor pleaded. "Show her what we can pay in exchange for royal sanction of our marriage."

"I'd rather have her set the price first. It may be less than we anticipate."

Almost as soon as he was ushered into her presence, however, he learned the price was much more than Father Anselem had predicted and Hugh had feared. Nor was the queen in any mood to haggle.

"You broke your holy vows," she snapped when he'd been ushered into her presence. "And you put aside the bride my husband, King Henry, approved for you."

Courtiers crowded her chamber. Pages scurried in and out. The archbishop of Westminster hovered almost at the queen's elbow, obviously anxious to conclude final arrangements for the coronation to take place on the morrow. Hugh was loathe to discuss his private affairs with the queen in such a public setting but had no choice.

"Lady Catherine and I together renounced those vows in front of a priest and witness."

"So Will Marshal informed me." The queen's lip curled. "How generous of the girl to let you go after all the years she was pledged to you. I hope you don't think to keep her dowry."

"I've promised to return it to her father," Hugh replied, keeping voice even and a tight rein on his temper. "Along with additional recompense to alleviate any affront to his honor."

"You return the dowry, but not the daughter?"

"Aye. Catherine wishes to join the Benedictine nuns at Chesire Piory."

The announcement put the queen at a distinct disadvantage. She herself served as royal patroness to any number of monasteries and abbeys, most notable the great abbey of Frontevraud in her beloved duchy of Aquitaine. She had already announced she would retire there when the time came, and desired to be buried there as well.

"Does the girl have a calling? Truly?"

"She does, and has stated as much to the priest who serves Exmoor. I've also pledged the Benedictines a rich gift for accepting Lady Catherine into their order," he informed the queen, then turned the discussion to the issue still hanging in the balance. "And I will pay whatever bride price you…or the king…deem appropriate for my lady wife."

That gave the queen pause. As the flamboyant young Duchess of Aquitaine, she'd established and presided over the famed Court of Love. Sophisticated and pleasure loving, the members of the court elevated the notions of chivalry and the pure, chaste love of a knight for his chosen lady to new heights. While some cynics suggested the love was not always chaste, the court's lofty decrees had spread far and wide over the years. So much so that the *chansons d'amour* composed by the queen's ardent followers were still the favorite of troubadours and poets.

Hugh caught an echo of those songs when the queen cocked her head and quizzed him. "So, Exmoor. You would beggar yourself for love?"

He smiled wryly. "I hope it doesn't come to that."

"And if it does?"

"Then," he replied with a shrug, "it does."

"She means so much to you, this Eleanor de Brac?"

"Aye."

They both knew King Richard could not risk completely disenfranchising the lords who held extensive lands in both England and on the Continent. As duke of Normandy, Aquitaine and Gascony, Count of Poitiers, Anjou, Maine, and Nantes, and overlord of Brittany, Richard needed loyal vassals to protect to his vast domains while he was on Crusade. That was why he'd pressed so many of them *not* to take the Cross. Why he demanded monies and men-at-arms from them instead. And why his mother now laid out the terms for his agreement to recognize the marriage of one of his wealthiest vassals.

"You will forfeit Bellemeade, Charlney, and Pontvieu to the crown," she announced. "And pay a fine of a thousand silver marks for daring to enter into a marriage contract without your liege lord's permission."

She read the outrage that flooded his face and flung up a warning hand. "These are the best terms I could wrest from my son, and only then because William Marshal added his voice to mine. Accept them, Exmoor, or you will find yourself in the Tower, your marriage nullified by the archbishop of Winchester, and *all* your lands forfeit."

His jaw tight, Hugh nodded.

"I'll have my chancellor draw up the necessary documents. You may sign them tomorrow, after you and the other senior vassals in attendance pledge allegiance to their new king."

Hugh used the time it took to wend his way back to his assigned chamber to clamp an iron fist around his emotions. When he relayed the terms to Eleanor in the privacy of their chamber, however, she gasped.

"Oh, Sweet Virgin! I'm so, so sorry, Hugh. Your lady mother told me Charlney came to you through your father, and his fathers before him."

"Aye. The grant goes back to the time of Denis Montmercy. He fought with Matilda, the countess of Anjou, in her battle to take the throne back from the usurper, Stephen of Blois."

Eleanor had scant interest in those long ago wars at the moment. Brushing them aside, she voiced another, more immediate concern. "Do you think the jewels in my casket will bring anywhere close to a thousand silver marks?"

"They should. If not, I'll visit one of the money lenders we spoke of at supper last night. In the meantime," he said with deliberate attempt to ease her worry, "we have a mummers' show, a joust, another banquet to attend before the coronation ceremonies tomorrow."

"Hugh! We cannot just…'"

"Nay, wife. No argumentation. What's done is done." Forcing a grin, he tipped her face to his. "I'm only hope I may not live to rue the day I took such a fiery-haired termagant to my bed."

She gave a reluctant laugh. "I hope so, too, husband."

Hugh followed the promised mummers' show, joust, and sumptuous banquet with a long and thoroughly satisfying session in his wife's arms. Mindful of the squires, pages and maids sharing pallets just a few feet away, he muffled his grunt when he slid into her. And Fulk's thunderous snores drowned her gasps, her pants, and her whispered words of love. His every muscle rigid with need, Hugh drove into her again, and yet again. With each thrust, he counted Charlney well worth the price of having Eleanor in his bed.

He left her early the next morning to attend the day-long coronation ceremonies. Eleanor's hair tumbled over her shoulders as she propped up on one elbow and grumbled yet again about the custom that barred women, children, and all unbelievers from the event.

"I'll wager that the queen finds a way to watch it."

"I wouldn't be surprised."

"Inscribe every sequence, every word in your mind, Hugh. I want a detailed account."

"You'll have it," he promised, dropping a quick kiss on her nose.

Richard's subjects displayed unbridled joy as the soon-to-be-king made his way from the Tower. The royal procession wound through Cheapside, home to London's busiest markets and merchants and halted several times to view extravagant pageants. Adding to the general exuberance was the wine that flowed freely through just-washed gutters.

The lusty cheers outside Winchester Cathedral alerted those within that the procession approached. The throng of nobles broke their various conversations and formed more orderly ranks. Hugh maneuvered into a spot with a clear view of the main aisle.

When Richard appeared, he looked little different from the warrior Hugh had fought alongside at the siege of Castillon-sur-Agen. At thirty-two, the duke was at the height of his physical powers. Taller than most, with reddish-blonde hair and the air of one well used to command, he followed a parade of prelates and his most senior nobles bearing a golden sword, spurs, cups, candles, and the royal scepter said to contain a fragment of the True Cross.

He knelt at the altar, surrounded by the bishops and abbots and holy relics, and swore a solemn oath that he would all the days of his life observe peace, honor, and reverence towards God, the Holy Church, and its ordinances. He also swore he would exercise true justice and equity towards the people committed to his charge. And that he would abrogate bad laws and unjust customs, if any such had been introduced into his kingdom, and would enact good laws, and observe the same without fraud or evil intent.

Having so sworn, he stripped down to his shirt and breeches for the anointing. Baldwin of Exeter, the Archbishop of Canterbury, poured holy oil on his head, his chest, and his right arm, which would wield a sword to the greater glory of God and England.

After the anointing, Richard donned consecrated linens and royal robes emblazoned with the arms of England. Golden spurs were attached to his boots, then he took the crown from the altar and handed it to the archbishop, who in turn placed it on his head.

The anointing done, the new king seated himself in a throne set on a high dais and received a solemn oath of allegiance from all the lords and barons present. Hugh's voice rose with the others, although a cynical corner of his mind couldn't help but wonder how many of those present would actually hold to that oath.

A joyous Mass of thanksgiving followed, after which the archbishops escorted the king from the cathedral. While the rest of crowd exited the cathedral and made for the palace, the new king changed into lighter robes and a crown that didn't press as heavily on his forehead. But almost as soon as he sat down to the planned, sumptuous did word begin to circulate of unrest in the city. It was a mere rumor at first. Some wealthy Jews, it seemed, unaware of the edict barring them along with all women, children, and other nonbelievers, had traveled to Winchester to present costly coronation gifts to their new king.

"My squire says they were stripped and flogged and driven away," the lord seated next to Hugh related. "He says, too, that word of the incident has spread like summer fire throughout the city."

And with it, the assembled celebrants soon learned, had spread the blood-chilling rumor that the new monarch had ordered all Jews murdered, their property confiscated, and their houses burned to the ground. There was looting and pillaging throughout London's Jewish quarter, with many inhabitants already massacred.

His face contorted with anger, Richard issued a swift order to the man he'd trained under, warred against, been taken prisoner by, and respected more than any other. "Marshal! Take what men you need and assist the Constable of the Tower to quell this mayhem."

"Aye, lord."

The big, battle-scarred warrior wasted no time. He left the high table and strode to the exit, booming out a shout as he went. "Granville. D'Marche! Exmoor! To me!"

The three pushed from the table and got their orders on a near run.

"Retrieve your armor, summon your men-at-arms, and assemble in the courtyard."

They took time only to send word to their men before rushing to retrieve their own arms. In his haste, Hugh took a wrong turn in the rabbit warren of halls and chambers. Cursing, he backtracked and found the familiar corridor and the right room.

Eleanor was relating some tale to an obviously enthralled group that included Fulk's lady, the maids, the squires and pages. No doubt telling them of flying carpets, Hugh guessed. His abrupt entry had them throwing him startled glances and brought his wife surging to her feet.

"What's amiss?" Before he could answer, she seized on the matter uppermost in her mind. "Have you spoken to the king? Has…Has he demanded yet more of you?"

"He has, but not what you think. I don't have time to explain all. Just that riots have broken out in the city, and I'm to assist the Marshal in subduing them."

Thomas, well trained squire that he was, leaped for the chest holding his lord's armor while Hugh thrust off the furred-and-embroidered mantle he'd worn to the coronation. Once he'd donned his gambeson and chain mail, he pulled on a surcoat prominently emblazoned with the eagle of Exmoor so his men could find him if it came to battle. Thomas helped Hugh strap on on his spurs and sword before he, too, scrambled into his gear. Wedging his helm under his arm, Hugh dropped a swift kiss on Eleanor's lips.

When he and Thomas rushed out into the courtyard, the September afternoon was still warm with the lingering heat of autumn but carried an acrid stink of woodsmoke. Praying it was from the castles kitchens and not a city already afire, Hugh leaped onto a mounting block to scan the milling horsemen for sight of his men. They'd not yet arrived from the field where they'd been bedded down. Nor had Granville's, he saw. But Marshal's high rank had guaranteed his men space in the castle and their mounts stalls in the royal stables. D'Marche's troop, too, must have been quartered closer in. The courtyard rang as nigh onto fifty horses stamped iron-shod hooves and battle axes and pikes clattered.

The noise doubled as another troop rode through the gate. Not Granville's, Hugh saw with a quick glance. Nor his own. Swallowing an oath, he recognized instantly the black wolf on the pennant flying from a pike staff.

Penhammond halted his troop just inside the yard and surveyed the scene with some surprise. When his glance fell on Hugh, surprise gave way to dislike. Making no effort to disguise it, he maneuvered his mount through the masses and drew rein beside the mounting block.

"Why are armed men assembling? Is an attack imminent?"

"You would know, Penhammond."

"God's bones, man! Do you think I would appear with such a small force if I was part of a planned assault?"

"I think you would dare whatever furthers your ends." Hugh's eyes narrowed. "Why do you come now, having so conveniently missed swearing fealty to the new king?"

"Bandits," the baron spit out. "A veritable army of them. They butchered a dozen pilgrims, then led us into swampy ambush when we gave chase. I lost two men battling our way out, and two days on the road. Now swallow your bile, Exmoor, and tell me…"

He broke off, his glance caught by the flutter of a shield with gold on one side, green on the other, with red lion rampant in the middle.

"The Marshal? He's here?"

"As you see."

"Word is Chester came as well."

Hugh didn't bother to respond. Penhammond had obviously dithered long over his decision whether to show himself, and had come only after the great Marcher lords had thrown their lot in with Richard.

The clatter of more arrivals drew attention. Sorocco's milk white mane was as unmistakable as his distinctive barding. Leaping off the mounting block, Hugh made for his men.

Chapter Eighteen

The Marshal sent outriders ahead to clear the way through the throngs of merrymakers celebrating the coronation along the Strand. The outriders scattered the merry makers but the armed troops still had to maneuver around the pie-makers' carts and ale-sellers' wagons that had been tipped and shoved haphazardly aside. Once into the city, the troop encountered even denser crowds. Some were still celebrating. Others had turned to rampage.

London's Jewish quarter, known as the Old Jewery, ran north to south from Gresham to Poultry Street. Within its precincts, the wealthier merchants, goldsmiths, and financiers had built grand mansions of stone while others had homes above their shops. Flames already leaped from the roofs of several mansions, and unruly mobs surged from house to house. Spilled chests and broken furniture littered the narrow lanes. Several bodies were sprawled in frozen horror, and a number of severely wounded lay groaning and crying for help.

Twisting in his saddle, Marshal roared his commands. "D'Marche, clear Honey Lane. Granville, you have Bread Street. Exmoor, with me! We'll push through to the Great Synagog before it, too, is ransacked."

The rioting crowds were afoot and would've stood little chance against a charge of mounted knights if the streets were not so narrow and twisting. Even worse, the many side lanes offered more chances to loot and pillage and murder. Another shouted command from Marshal sent one of his lieutenants and his men to chase the rabble on Milk Street. At the Marshal's shout, Hugh wheeled Sircocco and went after another, even larger, mob rampaging down Goldsmiths Row.

Building on both sides of the row were already aflame. Broken glass and shattered doors littered the cobbles. Hugh spotted more bodies, some hacked into pieces, as he plunged into the mob, laying the flat of his sword along side heads when he could, the honed edge when he could not. Those at the rear of the crowd shouted in alarm, but those at the front were too intent on murder and plunder to heed them. The mass surged forward, fell back, pushed forward again. All the while, flames roared and embers danced on the air above their heads.

The mounted troop plowed through the struggling mass. The looters' shouts and screams now echoed their victims. They fled down alleys when they could, flattened themselves against walls when they could not. Hugh was still laying about with the flat of his sword when he spotted a ruffian dragging a woman from a burning house by her hair. The brute was laughing, the woman screaming and kicking and crying for mercy. Another looter followed hard on their heels. This one dangled a red-faced, squalling infant by one foot. With a vile oath, Hugh spurred Sirocco and mowed down several rioters to reach the perpetrators.

He was still some yards away when another knight crashed through the crowd from a side street. He felled the oaf dragging the woman with one blow and had turned to deal with the one dangling the babe when the burning upper story their house gave way. The timbers collapsed in a whoosh of heat and flames, burying the knight, the woman, the babe, and the rioters.

With another curse, Hugh flung himself out of the saddle. His squire and those men close enough to see what was happening leaped down as well. Wielding swords and pikes and battle axes, they cleared enough of the burning timbers to reach the victims.

Hugh bent low to dodge the flames and half-dragged, half-carried the woman to safety. The other knight had tucked the babe in a fold of his surcoat and burst out of the death trap as well. The pillagers scrambled out last and were met with brutal blows from the disgusted men-at-arms. Only after they'd all retreated a safe distance from the flames did Hugh see the snarling black wolf on the other's scorched and soot-blackened surcoat.

"Christ's bones, Penhammond! Had I known it was you, I might have left you to the flames."

The baron was even less pleased to learn the identity of his rescuer. His mouth twisting, he thrust the babe into the arms of its frantic mother. "*Jesu,* Exmoor. I would as lief cut off my nose as be beholden to you."

"Do it! God knows it would improve your ugly phiz."

It might have been the heat of battle. Or the fellowship of arms. Or the absurdity of the Hugh's retort. Whatever the cause, both men broke into grins.

"I suppose the scales are even now," Penhammond said with voice made hoarse by smoke. "I can't skewer you after all for stealing my bride."

"And here I was, all aquake."

A shrill scream jolted them back to the mayhem still raging in the streets.

"We'd best to horse and be done with this business." Hugh thrust one foot in the stirrup. "Will you have one of your men take the woman and babe to safety?"

"I'll see to it. Have a care," the baron couldn't resist shouting after him, "or your widow might yet warm my bed."

The pillaging raged for several more hours, until the combined forces of the Constable of the Tower and those led by William Marshal beat down, rode down, or otherwise subdued the rioters. The fires raged even longer, but by midnight the citizenry had organized enough to use grappling hooks, ropes and axes to pull down burning thatch and timbers, then douse the flames with buckets of water.

When Hugh led his troop back to the field where they were quartered, he personally checked each man to ascertain the severity of their wounds. One had suffered blistering burns to his leg and hip when his leather breeks caught fire. Another had been struck in the throat by a hurled rock but he wheezed defiant assurances that he would be back in the saddle, ready to ride, whenever his lord said the word.

"Good man. But rest now, and I'll send a physician to you forthwith."

Eleanor had spent the long evening pacing and fretting. Lord Fulk returned from the extended coronation festivities to inform her and his own lady that the rioting was worse than first reported.

"The good Lord only knows how many buildings in the city are ablaze. Richard is sending more of us to help the Constable of the Tower contain the blaze."

Fulk had his squire arm him and kissed his wife farewell, leaving the two women and their attendant pages to worry as hour after hour dragged by. Eleanor recited more tales from the East, then read aloud from her psalter.

Midnight came and went. Fulk's lady took to her bed. Eleanor couldn't sleep and spent the long hours until dawn in prayer. She heard cocks crow and the sound of the castle stirring to meet the day when her husband and his squire at last returned.

"Hugh! Your face!"

He'd removed his helm and looked for all the world like one of the strange, tufted birds Eleanor had seen once in Jerusalem's marketplace! White across the forehead and down the slope of his nose where the helm had protected him, black everywhere it hadn't.

Surging to her feet, she rushed across the room. "Are there burns under all that dirt?"

"Mayhap one or two."

"Sit down and let me tend to you!"

The sleepy pages had already jerked awake. Eleanor set one scurrying to fetch clean water, another running to the kitchens for eggs and vinegar. While she rummaged in their traveling chest for her oiled packet of herbs and ointments, she threw a quick look at Thomas. The squire was as begrimed as his lord.

"Are you hurt?"

When he shook his head, she instructed him to help her undress Hugh. The scorches on his gauntlets made her gulp, as did those on her husband's surcoat. Obviously, both he and his squire had come closer to the fires either would admit.

Fearful of opening any blisters that might be under the soot, Eleanor took great care washing his face. The raw, weeping flesh she uncovered on his left cheek sent her stomach to her slippers.

Fulk's lady was wide awake now, too, and had thrown a mantle over her shift. "What medicants do you have in your packet?" she asked Eleanor urgently.

"Rose oil, lavender and comfy. Combined with vinegar and eggs, they form a poultice much used in the East."

"I have some milk of poppies. You must add that, too, to ease the pain."

"I don't need poppies' milk," Hugh protested. "The pain's not…"

"Be still," Eleanor snapped, strung tight by the sight of that oozing burn, "and don't show yourself more of a sapskull than you already have."

Fulk's wife gasped, Thomas snickered, and Hugh grinned.

"Remind me to beat you later, fishwife."

"Oh, certs. I'll be sure to do so. Now be still."

She was still bathing the wound when the page she'd sent for eggs and vinegar returned. He brought with him a tall, spare gentleman who introduced himself with a small bow.

"I am Robert FitzOsborne, physician to his majesty, the king. He's received reports of the action in the city, including one that your lord may have taken an injury."

"Indeed he has."

She moved aside to give him access to the patient. The fact that Hugh didn't protest told her that he knew well how easily burns festered and turned deadly. She hovered close while FitzOsborne bent to examine the raw, seeping flesh. To her relief, the physician saw no need to conduct a blood-letting. Instead, he swiped his forefinger across the burn and rubbed its ooze between finger and thumb to test its liquidity. He also approved the ingredients for Eleanor's compress.

"Apply it twice daily," he advised, "and keep him to a diet of beet soup, barley bread, and ale for at least a week. No wine, as it adds high humours to the blood."

Hugh grimaced, but Eleanor quelled him with a stern look. "We thank you, Sir Robert. Please convey our thanks to the king, as well."

"I will, indeed."

"I dislike beet soup," Hugh grumbled when the door closed behind the physician. "It tastes like beetle dung."

Eleanor ignored him as she tore the comfy and lavender into bits, then stirred them into the beaten eggs. Adding just enough vinegar, rose oil and poppies milk to form a thin paste, she carefully, gently spread the mixture over his burn. Her second best shift provided long strips of linen to bandage his cheek.

Marshal arrived just as she was tying the bandage in place. His surcoat and mail, too, were soot-darkened and stained. Eleanor felt Hugh brace himself for the bluff warrior's customary hammer blow of greeting but for once the Marshal restrained himself.

"I just saw Penhammond," he informed Hugh. "He's brought some woman and her babe back from the city."

"We came upon her at almost the same time. A looter was dragging her out of her burning home. Another was about to dash her babe's brains on the cobbles. The house fell around them, and it took both Penhammond and me to get them free of the flames."

Marshal nodded, well aware of the violence too often done to women during unbridled rioting. "He seems at a loss to know what to do with the female. She's clinging to him like a limpet."

As reluctant as Eleanor was to do Penhammond any good turn, she felt a sharp jab of pity for the woman and her child. "If he can't find other shelter, he could bring them to me."

"I'll send a page to tell him so. So Exmoor, are you fit enough to speak with the king?"

"Now?"

"Aye. He's sent word that he wants to see me, along with you and Granville. He would have our first hand account of what occurred."

"Of course. Thomas, a clean mantle."

Eleanor swallowed her instinctive protest as her husband pushed to his feet. She'd wiped away most of his grime, but his hair lay sweaty and as dark as old wood against his head. His eyes showed more red than blue from smoke, and the linen bandage swathed half his face.

When the door closed behind them, she was left once again to worry and wait.

Granville was waiting when Hugh and the Marshal were shown into one of Westminster's many small antechambers. "Christ's toes, Exmoor. You look like a scalded pig."

"Ha! At least I still have some hair on my face."

Or did he? A quick feel assured Hugh he didn't sport the same, brow-less look of surprise as Granville.

"How many men did you lose?" Marshal wanted to know.

"Only one," Granville reported with a moue of disgust. "The fool thrust his pike into a looter and let the carcass drag him from his horse. He was trampled underfoot by my own men."

"And you, Exmoor?"

"None, although one has a crushed throat that may yet strangle him. Any count on the number of Jews and looters killed?"

"Ten Jews that I know of. The Constable said a goodly number managed to escape and find safety in the Tower. As for the looters…"

His careless shrug indicated little concern for their fate.

They soon learned, however, that Richard didn't share his marshal's disregard for the miscreants. When they were ushered into his presence, he was closeted with the Archbishop of Canterbury, the Lord Chancellor, several scribes, and another lord Hugh couldn't put a name to. Richard showed few signs of having spent two nights doing penance, a long day in ceremony, and another night hosting elaborate celebrations. He greeted Marshal with a nod, Granville with a word of their fathers' close ties, and Hugh with a reminder of the final days of siege of Castillon-sur-Agen.

"As I recall, Exmoor, you and your men were first over the north curtain wall."

"While you and yours were storming the west wall, Sire."

The king nodded and requested detailed accounts the riot. When Marshal and the others finished, he swore and loosed the rein on his anger. He may have inherited his mother's sophistication and poetic bent, but his legendary temper was all Angevin.

"I want those responsible for this massacre drawn and quartered!" His rage was all the more potent for being as cold as ice. "They've desecrated my coronation. Now chroniclers down through the ages will claim it was stained with blood. My enemies will say the same. Particularly that puling pissant, Phillip of France."

None of those present displayed the least shock or surprise at his characterization of the French king. Most of the lords, including Richard, owed Phillip vassalage for their various holdings in France. And they all, *especially* Richard, considered the Capetan king more sly and cunning than honorable or brave.

"We've rounded up a goodly number of rioters," Marshal informed the king. "I misdoubt they were the instigators but they'll provide a nice feast for the crows."

"Make their deaths public and painful! A grim warning to others that I will not tolerate such violence against any of my subjects." He sucked in several breaths and drew rein on his temper. "Betimes, I will meet with the rabbi of London and heads of the most senior Jewish houses. It's the least I can do, seeing as they've pledged enough gold to arm and pay transport for two hundred of the knights who'll accompany me on Crusade."

None of his listeners thought it the least surprising that nonbelievers would fund a Christian war. The Jews, along with the Knights Templar were, after all, bankers and financiers to every king and great lord in Christendom.

"I owe you my thanks for this night's work," the king said. "More than my thanks. Marshal, I've already agreed you may wed your pretty little heiress. You'll take the title of Earl of Pembroke, as well."

A flush of pleasure suffused the great man's cheeks. He would've dropped to a knee in thanks but Richard stilled him.

"We go too far back for that, old friend. You may think I do you honor, but in truth I'm counting on you and my mother to hold my lands and kingdom together while I'm on Crusade. And keep my brother John in check," he added drily.

"You may count on me for both tasks, Sire."

"And you, Granville. Drummond Keep is yours, if you can wrest it from the Irish robber baron who holds it."

"Consider it taken, Sire."

By the time those cool gray eyes turned to the third in their party, Hugh had begun to hope his decision to wed Eleanor de Brac would not, after all, be the ruin of them both.

"My mother the queen tells me you repudiated your betrothal vows to Catherine of Langmont."

"Lady Catherine and I obtained a a writ of *quidquid voverat atque promiserat*, Sire. Together, we dissolved our vows."

The king frowned but it was the Archbishop of Canterbury who asked sharply. "Who approved such a writ? Where was it done? Not in Chester, surely. That bishopric is vacant."

"Since it *is* vacant, the writ was issued by an ordained priest and signed by witnesses, the Marshal among them."

The archbishop would've challenged the writ's validity further, but the king cut him off. "Take note, my lord Archbishop, and remember this when I end my betrothal to Princess Alys."

The churchman subsided, but all could see he thought the matter of ending a royal betrothal far more consequential than that of a mere baron. End it Richard would, though. Hugh didn't doubt it for a moment.

"My mother tells me also that the woman you've taken to wife has a spirit to match her own." The quick smile that came so rarely and held so much charm lifted one corner of Richard's mouth. "If so, I wish you luck bringing her to heel."

"I'll need it," Hugh returned dryly.

The smile faded. "I had decided to make you pay, and pay mightily, for daring to wed without our sanction."

"So your lady mother informed me."

"In recognition of your service last night, however, you may keep Charlney and Bellemeade. Pontvieu will revert to the crown."

The Marshal grunted a protest but Hugh was so relieved to retain his ancestral lands that he merely nodded. "As you will, Sire."

"I'm also reducing your fine from one thousand to five hundred silver marks. I would dispense with it altogether but I cannot allow my nobles to marry who and when and where they will without the crown's sanction. From what my mother says, you should be able to raise the sum readily enough. According to the her, you have a wife whose price is above rubies."

"Aye, Sire, I do."

"Now get you gone. All of you. After last night's exertions, you need sleep. And a bath," he added with another of his quick grins. "You stink of sweat and smoke."

Jubilant, the three detoured to the Marshal's spacious quarters to celebrate. Lolling in masculine comfort, they satisfied their hunger with a great platter of bread and meats washed down with several flagons of ale. An hour or more passed while they relived the events of the night just past and their meeting with the king.

Hugh was the first to lumber to his feet. "Eleanor's no doubt afire with impatience to hear what's transpired," he said with a touch of guilt.

"Aye, you'd best go to her," Marshal replied, grinning. "And take care that she doesn't peel the skin off the other side of your face for letting her stew so long."

Bracing for just such a storm, Hugh stopped outside the door to their shared chamber to draw a steadying breath. The effort pulled at the scored flesh under his bandage and made him wince. And the scene that greeted him when he opened the door made him halt on the threshold in surprise.

Half of London, or so it seemed, had crowded into the small chamber. Fulk, his lady, his squire and pages. Hugh's squire, Eleanor, their pages. Two strange women, one of whom occupied his bed and one who sat nursing a baby at her bared breast.

And Penhammond, curse him. Sprawled in a chair, legs outstretched, ale cup in hand, looking for all the world as though he were lord of the manor.

"Hugh! At last!" Eleanor flew to his side. "I'd begun to fear you'd been taken to the Tower."

"She feared," Penhammond drawled. "I hoped."

"Tell me!" Eleanor demanded, ignoring the deliberate provocation. "What said the king?"

Before he could answer, the woman on the bed gave a loud exclamation. Scrambling off the bed, she flung herself across the room to sank to her knees at at Hugh's feet. "I thank you, Sir, from the depths of my soul."

He'd caught barely a glimpse of her when he'd dragged her from the flames. At the time, her face had been too contorted by fear to show its truly astounding beauty. He could see it now in eyes so violet they reminded him of a deep, still lake at eventide. See it as well in her creamy skin and full, red lips that trembled as she poured out her thanks.

"I'll offer prayers of thanksgiving for you thrice daily, every day. As will my father. And his father, a man of great holiness. We'll all give thanks for you and for Baron Penhammond."

"Yes, well, God knows we need prayers. Penhammond more than I," Hugh added sardonically as he reached down to help her rise. "Did you take any serious hurt in the fire? You or your babe?"

"None that will not swiftly heal. But the babe isn't mine, Sir. He's the son of my sister, who died giving birth to him. Your lady was kind enough to search out a wet nurse for him while we waited for you to return."

Which explained the other woman sitting placidly with the infant to her swollen, blue-veined breast.

"You must allow my father to thank you in person, Sir. He and my grandfather were from home, thanks be to God, when the riots broke out. They'll return immediately, I know, when they hear of the trouble in the city. Please, allow them to seek you out. Or come to our shop in Goldsmiths' Row, if it still stands. If not, just ask for the direction of my father, Benjamin

Baruch. Or my grandfather, David Baruch. They'll gift you and your lady...and Baron Penhammond...most generously, I promise."

Hugh couldn't help but think of the heavy fine hanging over him. He wouldn't ask for or accept so great a gift, of course, but mayhap the Baruch's would pay a decent price for Eleanor's rubies.

But first...

He swept a quick glance over the crowded chamber. None of the occupants, including Penhammond, showed the least inclination to depart.

Exasperated, Hugh grasped Eleanor's upper arm. "Come, lady wife. I would have a word with you. In private."

With the castle still full to overflowing, they had to traverse the almost the full length of the corridor before they found an unoccupied window niche. Sunbeams cut like bright swords through the wavy glass and showed the tired lines in Eleanor's face. But her green eyes were bright and eager as she demanded a recounting.

"Tell me! What said the king?"

"He said he wished me luck taming the termagant I've taken to wife."

"Hugh! Don't fash with me. Truthfully, what did he say?"

"I swear, it's true. He said the queen told him that you have a spirit to match hers. He wished me luck bringing you to heel."

Her mouth dropped. Hung open a moment. Then shut with a snap. Fire leaped into her eyes, so fierce it might well sear off the rest of his skin, just as the Marshal had predicted.

"That's *all*? You did naught but trade insults about me with the king?"

"He also resorted to the Holy Scripture."

"What? You prayed together? You and the king?"

Laughing, he took pity on her surprise, irritation and utter confusion. "Richard quoted from Proverbs, reminding me I have a wife whose price is above rubies. And once again, I could only agree."

"Oh. Well."

Still grinning, he tugged on a strand of flame red hair still disordered from her long, sleepless night. "Your pretty stones don't hold half the fire you do. Or one tenth the worth. You, my fair and fearsome Eleanor, are indeed beyond price."

Bending, he claimed her mouth with his.

THE END

Author's note

As Richard predicted, the history of his coronation is, indeed, tainted by violence that marred it. Sadly, the violence grew worse once he left for the Crusades. Without his restraining hand, the collective hatred for all non-believers fanned by the religious fervor of Crusades grew worse. Added to that was the animosity of English barons who had put themselves heavily in debt to successful Jewish bankers and traders.

In the weeks following Richard's departure, arson, vandalism, and massacres occurred all across England. Attacks took place in Lynn Colchester, Stamford, and Thetford. Jews in Lincoln saved themselves only by taking refuge in the city's castle. The worst attack occurred on the 16th and 17th of March, 1189, in the city of York. An estimated one hundred and fifty died in the pogrom, which eradicated York's entire Jewish community.

In an ironic twist of fate, when Richard was captured and held for ransom on his voyage home from the Crusades, his mother turned to Jewish leaders for help raising the exorbitant sum demanded for his release.